JAXON

DADDIES OF PINE HOLLOW
BOOK 1

KATE OLIVER

This book is a work of fiction. Names, characters, organizations, places, events, and incidents are either a product of the author's imagination or are used fictitiously. Any resemblance to actual persons, living or dead, businesses, companies, events, or locales is entirely coincidental.

Written by: Kate Oliver
Cover Designer: Scott Carpenter

Copyright © 2023 Kate Oliver

"ALL RIGHTS RESERVED. This book contains material protected under International and Federal Copyright Laws and Treaties. Any unauthorized reprint or use of this material is prohibited. No part of this book may be reproduced or transmitted in any form or by any means, electronic or mechanical, including photocopying, recording, or by any information storage and retrieval system without express written permission from the author/publisher."

CONTENT WARNINGS

This book is a Daddy Dom romance. The MMC in this book is a Daddy Dom and the MFC identifies as a Little. This is an act of role-playing between the characters and falls under the BDSM umbrella. This is a consensual power exchange relationship between adults. The MFC uses a pacifier, bottle, and wears training panties. In this story there are spankings and discussions of other forms of discipline.

Please do not read this story if you find any of this to be disturbing or a trigger for you.

1

LEAH

"What do you think, Buttercup? Isn't it beautiful?"

My passenger doesn't respond, but I probably shouldn't expect her to—considering she's a stuffed bear. Still, I can see from the sparkle in her little plastic eyes that she loves it. Okay, maybe the sparkle in her eyes is actually the glitter making up the color of her irises, but I'm going to take what I can get right now.

I stare at the small but perfect house before me and smile. This is my new beginning, and it's gorgeous. It's everything I could ever want. Sure, the roof needs some work, the plumbing might be a little iffy, and the walls have several holes that need to be patched, not to mention a few dozen other things throughout the house in need of attention. But I don't care. This house is all mine. Paid for in full. So instead of worrying about a mortgage, I can use my income for updates and repairs and make it exactly how I want it.

The movers will be here soon. It's going to be a long day. I can't even fathom how people move without a moving company. The guys that came and loaded up all my stuff are a freaking godsend. They aren't bad to look at either. Not that I'm looking. Sheesh. I just got out of a shitty marriage. The last thing I need is a man complicating my life. Doesn't mean I can't admire, right? So while I might look at the men who are moving all my stuff—heck, I might even think about them while I use my vibrator tonight—but that will be it. My battery operated boyfriend, Hercules, is all I need to satisfy my needs.

"What do you say, Buttercup? Want to go inside and have a tour?"

Even though she doesn't respond, I know she's just as excited about this move as me. Because of my ex, she had to sleep in the closet for the past several years. According to him, "grown women shouldn't sleep with stuffed animals." Whatever. Who ever said I was a grown woman? He knew I was Little when he met me. He thought he could change me. Mold me into the perfect little housewife. No, thank you. I don't want to be a housewife. I like my job, and I like being Little. I'm just glad I got out when I did and refused to conform to the box he wanted to put me in. It's one of the only times I've been glad my body is broken.

I reach over and unbuckle Buttercup from her seat—safety first, duh—then get out of the car with her tucked under my arm. It's a bit chilly outside, and I probably should have worn a jacket. I was just too excited this morning, I couldn't be bothered with one. It *is* November, though, and the weather is only getting colder by the day.

The trees have all turned those beautiful shades of gold and orange, making everything look like a fancy painting. Leaves crunch under my feet as I make my way up to the porch of my new home. It's like one of those feel good movies, and for once, I'm the star. I've needed something uplifting for so long, and other than the day the judge finalized my divorce, it's been too long since I've felt this happy.

Boards creak under my feet, and I'm careful to test the

strength of them before putting my full weight down. The last thing I want is to fall through a weak spot. That would be bad and very embarrassing. Thankfully, despite the groaning of the wood, it seems plenty sturdy to hold weight so it shouldn't be an issue for the movers.

It's musty inside, but I don't care. I'll burn candles in every room until the smell goes away. For now, I move from window to window and open each one to let in fresh air. Maybe that will help.

With Buttercup tucked under my arm, I walk through the rooms with a permanent smile on my face. The home is small. Only about fifteen hundred square feet. Not even half the size of the house I shared with my ex-husband. There are three bedrooms and two bathrooms. The kitchen, dining room, and living room are one big open space. It was the first thing I fell in love with when I walked in. I can already picture where I'll put my Christmas tree. I'll be able to see it while I'm in the kitchen or the living room. It's perfect. And it's all mine.

Even though I haven't moved a single belonging into this house yet, it already feels more like home than the house I shared with Kevin. The house we had was nearly four thousand square feet, and everything was pristine and brand new. I never felt at home there.

I force those memories out of my mind. Today is a new day and a fresh start, and the last thing I should be thinking of is my asshole ex. Sometimes I get so mad at myself for letting him take up space in my head, but when you've been married to someone for so long, their words and actions become so ingrained in your mind it's hard to forget. It will take time to heal from the wounds he caused, but I'm already feeling so much better than I was a month ago. Our divorce has been final for nearly six months and each month has gotten better and better. I can hardly wait to see where I am a year from now.

A truck horn sounds from the driveway. I smile and leave Buttercup on the kitchen counter so I can greet the movers and start directing them where to put everything. It's going to be a long day of unpacking, but this is the first day of the rest of my life and I can hardly wait.

2

JAXON

"Who're the new neighbors?" I can't stop myself from rolling my eyes at Silas' dumbass question. "How the hell should I know? They just started moving in."

Silas, my best friend, shrugs as he leans down and pats my dog's head. "I thought you might have met them when they came for the inspection or something."

You would think the fact that we've been friends practically all our lives would mean the idiot knows I'm not exactly the neighborly type of guy. Hell, I've lived in this house for five years and I don't know a single one of my neighbors' names. After the first six months, they stopped knocking on my door with casseroles and "get to know ya" pies. It's not that I'm an asshole. Okay, actually, I am kind of an asshole. But I'm just not a small-talk kind of guy. I keep to myself and I like it that way.

"Well, I didn't. I am curious who the inspector is, though. That fucking house is uninhabitable. The roof looks like a damn cheese grater and I'm pretty sure the entire thing is one big fire hazard."

I stand at my kitchen sink, watching the half dozen men

carrying boxes and furniture from the truck. Whoever's moving in better know what the hell they've gotten themselves into because that house is in shambles.

My friends are here for poker night, but we haven't started the game yet. We're still drinking beers and shooting the shit.

"You should have bought it, man. Fixed it up and rented it out. You could have gotten it for a steal," Linc says.

I grunt. I'd had serious thoughts about buying it. It was priced way below market average because of the condition it was in. I could have easily fixed it up good as new and turned it into a rental for some extra cash. For some reason, though, every time I went to call my real estate agent to make an offer, something stopped me. My gut told me the house wasn't meant to be mine. My gut is rarely wrong, so I listened to it, and now some family is moving into the damn house before they repair it enough for it to be livable.

Shit. The last thing I need is more business. Sawyer Construction is already booked out a year in advance for jobs, but maybe I'll leave my business card on their doorstep just in case. It would be the neighborly thing to do, right? Yeah, fuck that. They can find their own contractor. I don't want people in my neighborhood showing up on my front step asking for favors.

"Are we playing poker or what?" Silas asks.

Everyone crowds around my dining room table with beers and snacks in hand. All of my best friends are here. This is the one social event I actually look forward to. Maybe it's because we're all so close, and they don't mind my grumpy ass. These guys are basically family to me. Then again, when you grow up in a small town like Pine Hollow, everyone feels like family. Or at least they treat you like you are. Until you're the center of a scandal and they feel like they need to choose sides.

"I'll deal," Asher offers.

Jaxon

I sit back and take a drink of my beer. "Give me something I can work with, Ash-hole."

Asher flips me off as he passes out cards. As soon as I look at my hand, I let out a groan and immediately fold.

"We need to plan a trip to Twisted," Cole says.

"Need to get laid, Morgan?" Dane asks with a smug grin on his face.

Cole grins. "I'm pretty sure we all do. How long has it been for you fuckers? I don't even know that I need to get laid. I just need something fun and soft to Daddy a little bit."

I let out a grunt. It's been way too long since I had sex—or anything resembling sex—with something other than my hand. Cole is right, though. It's not the sex I need. It's the other part. Playing the Daddy role. Finding a sweet Little girl to take care of, even if it's just for a night. Because that's all it can be with me. One night. That's all I can give of myself.

"Let's plan it," I say.

Everyone nods in agreement. Twisted is a BDSM club forty minutes outside of Pine Hollow. It has a huge section specifically for age players and caretakers. Every so often, we plan an overnight trip where we hit the club and stay in a nearby hotel.

Almost always, we each find a Little to play with for the night. Well, Linc and Gage play with one together but the rest of us don't share. I unwillingly shared my ex for years and won't do it again. Not that it matters since I also refuse to ever get involved long-term again after the shit I went through with Wendy. No, thank you. I'll settle for one-night stands for the rest of my life to fulfill that side of my life when I really need it.

"Anyone need another beer?" I ask.

Austin grins at me from across the table. "Are we going for shit-faced tonight?"

I shrug. I've already had two, but for some reason, the

topic of playing with a Little is making me want to drink more. I always get this way. I'm a fucking coward. Wendy ruined me for any type of relationship. Even letting myself get involved with someone for one night stresses me out. But, I need it. I need to Daddy someone. I need to feel wanted and needed. Even if it's just a temporary fix.

"Shut up and deal," I reply as I grab more beers and pass them around.

FUCK. Why the hell did I drink so much? I'm forty-seven years old. Anything more than three beers in a night means I'll be hungover the entire next day. And that's exactly how I've spent my Sunday. Willie, my one-eyed pit bull, has spent the day sleeping on the couch with me. He's having the time of his life being lazy while my head has feels like it's being pounded by a jackhammer.

It was after two in the morning when I went to bed. A few of the guys crashed in my spare rooms but were gone by the time I woke up. I have a feeling they were probably feeling like shit too. My only hope is that by tomorrow when I have to work, I'll feel halfway human again.

When Willie starts nudging his dog bowl in the kitchen, I realize it's nearly dark out. I spent the entire damn day on the couch. I desperately need a shower and something to eat.

I force myself up and go to the kitchen to fill Willie's bowl. As soon as I set it in front of him, he dives in. Food flies everywhere. Even though I've had him for three years, he still has some of the scars, physical and mental, from his life before me. I can't blame him. He'd practically been skin and bones when I found him at the shelter. Even now, he still acts as though each meal might be his last.

While he eats, I throw on a hoodie and a pair of sneakers. I don't have the energy to cook anything, so I call in a pizza

Jaxon

order for pick up. Willie follows me out to my truck. As I pull out of my driveway, I notice a lamp on in the front window of the house next door. I can't see anyone inside, though.

Pepperoni Palace is only a short drive. Pretty much everything in this town is a five-minute drive. There are no stop lights here. No traffic. Everything is close by, and everyone knows everyone — as well as their personal business.

I'm so hungry I don't even wait to grab a slice and eat it on the way. Almost immediately I start to feel better. Maybe I should have eaten earlier. Or better yet, maybe I shouldn't drink more than three beers. You'd think at my age I'd have learned that lesson.

When I get out of my truck, Willie jumps out and jogs off in the opposite direction of the front door.

"Willie!" I call.

I hear a shriek and then a giggle. I round my truck and stop dead in my tracks when I see a bear. Not a real bear. A human dressed in a bear onesie, crouched down and rubbing my dog's ears like they're best friends.

"Aren't you a good boy? So cute."

The bear is obviously a woman based on her soft voice and, for some reason, my cock stirs in my sweats.

"Willie," I call.

He ignores me completely, but the woman looks up. Though it's almost dark out, the street lamp gives off just enough light to illuminate her face. Full lips, wide eyes, and an adorable little button nose.

"Oh, hi," she says.

She rises to her full height, which isn't much. She's got to be at least a foot shorter than me. And she's a sight to take in. Breathtakingly beautiful.

I grunt in response.

Her gaze moves from me to Willie and then back to me.

"I just moved in. You must be my neighbor. I'm Leah. Leah Day."

It's everything I can do not to let my eyes skim down her lush body.

"And you are?" she finally asks.

"Jaxon."

When I don't offer anything else, she smiles softly, looks at Willie, and lowers herself to his level again, scratching him behind his ears.

"Your dog is so sweet. He's a pit bull, right? Aw, he only has one eye. Poor boy. What's your name, buddy?"

She's a peppy little thing.

"Willie," I grunt. "His name's Willie."

Her hands freeze. Then, she starts giggling.

"You have a dog with one eye named Willie? You have a one-eyed Willie?"

She's practically shaking as she giggles. For fuck's sake. I need to change my dog's name now. How the fuck had I never put that together? Did the shelter name him that as some cruel joke? My dog is named after a fucking wiener? How fucked up is that?

"That was his name when I got him."

Willie seems to think she's the best thing since sliced bread and wiggles closer to her. Her lips roll in like she's trying to get control of herself, and I'm still trying to figure out why the fuck she's dressed like a bear.

"It's not Halloween," I finally say.

Her eyebrows pull together as she looks up at me. "What?"

"You're dressed like a bear."

The giggles start again as she looks down at herself. "Oh! I forgot I had this on. It's garbage night and I forgot to take out my bins earlier. I figured since it was dark out, no one would see me. How embarrassing."

Jaxon

When I don't say anything, she rises again and starts to back up into her driveway.

"Right, well, it was nice meeting you, Jaxon. And it was nice meeting your one-eyed Willie," she says. "Have a good night."

I'm left watching her disappear into her house, the nub of the tail on her bear costume moving with each sway of her hips. I'm totally watching her ass. My cock is practically at full salute, waving goodbye to her and her perfect, round ass. Fuck.

"Come on, dog. We need to figure out a new name for you," I say as I grab the pizza from my truck.

Willie looks toward my neighbor's house and lets out a dramatic sigh before he trots after me.

That woman was... I don't even know. Whoever her husband is, the man has his hands full, that's for sure. Note to self, avoid the new neighbors. No bears allowed.

3

LEAH

Great. Just freaking fantastic.
    Why me? Why?
    I do a little foot stomp once I've closed my front door. I really want to have a full-blown tantrum right now. Like throw myself on the floor and kick and scream.

Why is it that the first time I meet my insanely hot neighbor is when I'm in my freaking bear onesie? How humiliating! I had no idea I had a hot neighbor, and if I *had* known, I probably wouldn't have chanced going outside in this outfit, even in the dark. But noooo, of course he had to be good looking.

He looks like the type of man who works with his hands. Enormous and solid. He definitely has biceps I'd like to squeeze. And even though he grunts a lot, I find that kind of endearing. He seems a bit grouchy, but then again, I did point out that he basically named his dog after a penis.

Jeez. Nice going, Leah. Way to win the approval of my neighbors. He's probably telling his wife right now about how fat and pathetic I am.

Why did I have to be wearing this outfit? All my rolls

and my huge thighs and butt are basically on full display. I've never worn this onesie anywhere. It's a size too small, so it hugs everything. I'm pretty sure even my thigh dimples are visible. My boobs are practically bursting from the top like a can of biscuits, and it's a *bear*, for goodness sake.

I drop onto the couch and sigh. I don't know why I'm so upset. It's not like his opinion matters. He's just my neighbor. Okay, he's extremely hot, but that means nothing. The movers were also hot. There are plenty of hot guys out there. Granted, the movers hadn't gotten my blood flowing down there like Grunty McGrunterton had, but still.

Jaxon. That was his name. He looks like a Jaxon. Tall. Burly. A full beard that I kind of want to run my fingers through. I wonder what that thing would feel like between my thighs. My eyes widen at the thought. Jesus, Leah. Get it together. Stop being a horny little hussy.

His doggie was adorable, though. Even though he only had one eye and several scars on his face, he was as sweet as could be and I wouldn't mind snuggling him all night. At least the dog didn't seem to judge me for my outfit. It had been clear that McGrunterton hadn't approved, though.

"It's not Halloween."

Duh. It's November. Sheesh. My vagina must have been the only one thinking while we were out there because I'm just now realizing how rude Jaxon whatever-his-last-name-is was. The guy barely said a word. He was too busy being all caveman-grunt-this and caveman-grunt-that. Then again, I called his dog a penis.

Whatever. He seemed like the type of guy who would want nothing to do with his neighbors so it's unlikely that I'll ever have to talk to him again. I'll definitely never set foot outside my house in this onesie again. That's for dang sure.

I need wine to numb some of this embarrassment. I pry myself off of the couch and go to the kitchen. There are still boxes everywhere. Every surface is covered with random stuff. I've been focusing on getting my bedroom settled before I unpack anything else in the house. That way I have a cozy spot to escape and regress when I get overwhelmed.

I find a sippy cup and fill it with wine before I secure the lid and take a deep swallow of what I pretend is juice. Sometimes it really is juice, but tonight is definitely an adult beverage kind of night.

The rest of my evening is spent in my bedroom, unpacking stuffed animals and my other toys. I also hang curtains and organize my dresser and closet.

By the time I crawl into bed, I'm wiped and a little buzzed. I dig through my nightstand until I find my pacifier and slide it between my lips before I start the movie I'm going to fall asleep to. As it plays, though, my mind isn't on the movie. It's on the grumpy man who lives next door. For some strange reason, the thought of him soothes me until I fall into a peaceful slumber.

IT'S BEEN RAINING for four days straight. Not just a little rain. No, Mother Nature has sprung a leak, and I don't see it stopping anytime soon. I wouldn't mind it except I'd planned to walk to and from work so I could get some exercise. Oh, well. I'm getting plenty of a workout inside my own house.

The day after I met my neighbor, I painted the living room. Then I spent the next day on my hands and knees, scrubbing the filth out of the tiles in the kitchen. My arms are still sore. And of course, then there was a leak under the sink that went all over the kitchen floor. After three trips to The Rusty Screw hardware store and seven YouTube videos later, I fixed the leak and was quite proud of myself. Then I scrubbed the entire kitchen floor again.

After that, my shower knob broke, so I watched more videos and took more trips to the hardware store. I'm now the proud owner of a new shiny knob, and I even sprung for a new shower head which has one of those detachable wands. It's a lovely wand and might be quite useful one day.

I'm hoping tonight I'll be able to take a break from doing anything house related and will actually be able to regress for the entire night while eating chicken nuggets and watching a movie. I'm tired. I really need a break from things going wrong in my new home because, seriously, I might cry if something else breaks today. On top of that, this weather is making me feel a little blue. Of course it could also just be a side effect of my condition, but it's easier to blame it on the rain.

Warmth fills my chest when I pull into the driveway. I still have a long way to go before this place is where I want it to be, but it's home and I love it. With a quick glance toward my hot neighbor's house, I head toward my front porch. I haven't seen Jaxon since the night I embarrassed myself in my bear onesie.

Even though I'm not ashamed of my Little side, it's not something I'm used to showing others. The only times I've ever been in Little Space outside of my house are the few times I've gone to Twisted, but they were so long ago. I was with Kevin and things were still going well between us. So at least two years ago. Maybe I should look into joining the BDSM club again. Even though I'm not looking for a Daddy, I wouldn't mind making friends with some Littles.

When I walk into my bedroom to change out of my floral smelling work clothes into something comfy, I end up stopping in my tracks just inside the doorway.

"Oh, no, no, no! Oh, my Gosh!"

I rush over to my bed and start grabbing my stuffed toys, which are all soaked, and toss them to the other side of the room. Normally I wouldn't be so careless with them, but water is leaking through my freaking ceiling.

The inspectors told me the roof would need to be replaced in the near future, but I hadn't expected that to mean five days after I moved in. Crap. I need to get on top of the roof and cover it with a tarp or something.

I run to the garage, thankful the previous owners left a ladder. It looks rickety and a little scary, but it will do. It's heavy and awkward as I lug it outside and lean it against the gutters. I've never climbed on a roof before, but surely, it's easy. I'm going to have to see how big the hole is so I know what size tarp to ask for at the hardware store. I should probably see if they have a frequent buyer program there or something.

When I'm satisfied with how secure the ladder feels against the house, I start to climb. At the third step I look down and decide not to do that anymore because it was a really bad idea. I swear I feel the ladder shaking. Or maybe it's just me. I don't like heights. Nope, not at all.

It takes way too long for me to finally reach the top and when I do, I'm not sure if I want to actually climb onto the roof. Why did all those DIY shows I watched make things seem so easy? I was sure I could do this when I bought the house. I'd pretty much run everything at my other house when I lived with Kevin because he was always so busy with work or his flavor of the week. Then again, our house was practically new, so it didn't have any of the problems this house does.

With a deep breath, I awkwardly crawl onto the roof and get to my feet. Okay, that wasn't so bad. I won't think about how it's going to go when I have to get down. It would be really helpful if the rain would stop for just a little while until I'm no longer standing on top of my house.

Slowly, I walk toward the area of the roof just above my bedroom, but I can't see where the leak is coming from. Of course it won't be easy to find. Why can't it be an actual hole that I can see? As I take slow steps, I notice that some areas feel a little weaker than others, and I pray to everything I believe in that I don't have a *Christmas Vacation* incident where I end up going through the roof.

"Leah!" a male voice roars.

I glance back to see a very angry looking Jaxon stomping toward my house.

"What the hell are you doing up there?" he demands.

He's obviously feeling just as friendly as he was the other night. When he disappears from view, I'm unsure what to do until I hear him stomping up the ladder. A second later, his scowling face appears.

"What the fuck are you doing? It's pouring down rain and you're walking around your roof? Get over here."

Did he just scold me like a child? And demand I come to him? Sheesh, this man is ballsy. And really hot when he's scowling. What the heck is wrong with me? And who does he think he is?

"Do you think I'm up here for fun? I have a leak in my roof and I need to cover it. Go away, Jaxon. I don't need you here to yell at me while I try to figure this out. I'm a perfectly capable, independent, single woman, and I can figure out how to fix a leak."

His brief silence tells me he's surprised by my bluntness. I'm a little surprised by it too. I don't know why I announced that I was single. That's none of his business and has nothing to do with my roof. But this is my new start. Maybe it's a new me too. Although my trembling bottom lip is right on par with how I'd normally react to being scolded. Hopefully he can't see that through the rain.

"Jesus Christ, Leah. Get over here. It's not safe. I'll look at your roof, but for the love of God, get your little ass over here so I can help you down. I'm having a fucking heart attack."

Jaxon

Oh. Well, that was kind of sweet. Sort of. He thinks I have a little ass. Brownie points for him. He's worried about me in his own grumpy way. I'm not sure I know how to handle that. He's also offering to help me. Shouldn't I take him up on that? I saw the Sawyer Construction logo on the side of his truck, so he probably knows what he's doing. And if the cranky hottie wants to help me with this disastrous situation, it would be the neighborly thing to do to let him, right? I could make him cookies in return.

"It's dripping inside my house."

His expression is still granite. "Leah Day, get your ass over here. This roof is a goddamn death trap waiting to happen. So help me, if I have to come get you..."

I should probably be spitting mad that he's talking to me like this. That he's practically threatening me. But the ridiculous side of me is swooning because Grumpy McGrumperson is worried about me. With a roll of my eyes, I carefully walk to the edge of the roof.

"Well, I can't get down with you standing there."

He grunts and descends a couple of steps. "Turn around and put your hands on the sides of the ladder, then lower one foot onto the first rung. I'll stay right behind you to keep it steady."

I stare at him for a long moment. If I turn around and he's right behind me, my big ass is going to be right in his face. Ugh.

"I don't need you to stay on the ladder. I can get down by myself."

His brown eyes darken, and I'm pretty sure if it were possible, smoke would be coming from his ears. "I'm not moving. It's slippery and this ladder looks ancient. Do as I say."

With a huff, I turn around and slowly follow his instructions.

"Good girl. One step at a time," his deep gravelly voice says from right behind me.

My pussy clenches at the simple praise. I can't remember the last time I was called a good girl.

When I'm almost down, Jaxon wraps his hands around my waist and lifts me off. I let out a yelp of surprise as he sets me on the ground like I weigh nothing.

When I turn around to thank him, I freeze. He has his hands on his hips and he's scowling down at me.

"What in the world were you doing up there by yourself?"

I blink several times as I shake my head in disbelief. "I was trying to fix my roof, obviously. It's leaking into my bedroom. I can't sleep underwater. I'm not a mermaid."

His eye starts to twitch. I probably need to tone down the sass. He doesn't look like he's in the mood for it. Well, tough. I'm not in the mood to be scolded for trying to fix another disaster.

Maybe Kevin was right. Maybe I'm not smart enough to do this by myself. My shoulders drop and my bottom lip trembles. Jaxon notices and his scowl softens slightly. He runs one of his enormous hands over his face and sighs.

"Do me a favor. Go get my dog out of my truck and take him into my house. There are towels in the bathroom so you can dry off and there's a kettle in the pantry. Make yourself some tea. You're shivering. I'm going to go look and see what needs to be done to fix your roof."

When I hesitate, he lifts my chin with his index finger. "Go. Get some doggie snuggles and get warmed up. I'll be over in just a minute."

I don't want to listen to him. He's not my Daddy or my boyfriend or my husband, but at the same time, despite the terrible way he's getting his point across, he's trying to help me and maybe I need to accept some help once in a while.

After giving him a slow nod, I head toward his truck. As

much as I hate to admit it, even though I'm soaked from the rain, my panties are soaked for an entirely different reason and I'm not sure how to feel about that. If I'm totally honest with myself, I don't want to think about what it means because right now I just want to follow his instructions and hopefully hear those two little words from his lips again.

4

JAXON

I think I'm having heart palpitations. This woman is going to kill me, and I don't even know her. When I pulled into my driveway after work and found Leah up on the roof in the pouring fucking rain, I saw red.

Then, that plush little bottom lip had to tremble and make me feel like the biggest asshole alive for yelling at her. She's single. Why is it that out of all the things she said to me, those two words are sticking out the most?

As soon as she disappears with my dog, who, by the way, I'm no longer calling Willie, I make my way into her house. She said it was dripping inside, which is definitely a bad sign. Depending on how bad the leak is, it could cause the drywall ceiling to collapse.

The house is still a mess of boxes. When I find nothing in the living room or kitchen, I head down the hall and check each room. When I step into the last one, every bit of air rushes out of my lungs and I mutter, "Fuck." And now I know for a fact that I'm the biggest fucking asshole in all of Pine Hollow.

She's a Little. I should have realized it the night I saw her in that bear onesie when she couldn't stop giggling. I was too distracted by her beauty to realize what that onesie might have meant. But now, standing in the doorway of her bedroom, which is full of stuffed animals, a toy box, and a bookshelf filled with both chapter books and children's books, it's obvious what she is.

Maybe she has a kid I haven't seen? That would be a perfectly normal explanation. She could be a single mom. But based on the book on her nightstand called *Safe with Daddy*, plus the adult-size pacifier sitting right next to it, I think it's safe to say that Leah Day is a Little. And I don't know what to think about that.

My protective side is going all crazy, and I'm fighting the urge to go over to my house, put her over my knee, and spank her lush bottom for doing something so dangerous. The rational side of me is telling me to run for my life and get away from this woman I haven't stopped thinking about since the night I first laid eyes on her.

Shit! The dripping water from her ceiling brings me back to reality, and I go on the hunt for some kind of bucket. Her bed is soaked and, from the looks of it, her pile of stuffed animals thrown haphazardly on the other side of the room are wet too.

I pull out my phone as I continue to search for a bucket.

"Hey, Jax. What's up?" Silas answers.

"Are you still at the shop?"

Silas isn't only my best friend. He's also my lead foreman at Sawyer Construction.

"I was just getting ready to leave. You need something?"

Yeah. A fucking punch to the gut. Oh wait, it feels like I already got one when I discovered my adorable new neighbor is a fucking Little.

"Can you bring over a few big blower fans and some tarps? My neighbor has a leak in her roof."

Silas doesn't say anything for several seconds. "A leak in her roof, huh? Her husband isn't taking care of it?"

Jaxon

This is why small towns are a pain in the ass. Everyone fucking meddles and wants to know everyone's business. If it were anyone else besides Silas, I'd ignore him completely.

"According to her, she's independent and single. She was on top of her damn roof when I got home."

My friend whistles. "Damn. Is she cute? You think she could be interested in a Daddy to take care of her? I can help her out with fixing her place up and play house with her at the same time."

My friend talking about her that way makes me want to kick his ass. No one is going to Daddy her. Except me. Only that's not fucking happening. I don't Daddy women. Especially not women I'll see again. Maybe I should move.

"Bring me the stuff I need," I snap as I place a bucket under the drip.

Silas laughs, and I end the call. He's an asshole and I don't want to think about why what he said bothers me so much.

I spend the next twenty minutes being pissed off while I grab tarps from my garage. Her roof is going to need to be patched, but I have to wait until the weather clears so I can see how bad it is. From the looks of it, the entire thing needs to be replaced. I don't have the time for that. But damn those wide blue eyes and trembling bottom lip. Even though I don't have time, I'll make room in my schedule for her.

I'm soaked to the bone by the time Silas shows up. I don't want to show him Leah's room. That would just feed the bullshit he was spewing over the phone. If *anyone* is going to look out for her, it's going to be me. It's the neighborly thing to do, after all. Even I roll my eyes at myself over that thought. Since when have I ever given a shit about my neighbors?

Silas stares up at her roof with a scowl on his face. "She was walking up on that roof? Fuck. The woman is just asking to get hurt."

I let out a grunt of agreement.

Leah emerges from my house with a mug of tea in her hand. Her hair is still wet, and she looks exhausted. I want to wrap her up in a blanket. I'm not going to, but the urge is there.

"Hi," Silas says as he crosses our driveways to reach her.

Silas is my opposite in every way. He's charming and funny. I'm charming in an Oscar the Grouch kind of way. I don't even want to think about which one of us she'd be more attracted to because I have no doubt it wouldn't be me.

"Hi. I'm Leah," she says sweetly.

My friend holds out his hand. "Nice to meet you, Leah. I'm Silas Ward. I'm friends with Jax."

She shoots me a glance before shaking Silas' hand. "Nice to meet you too. I didn't think Jaxon had any friends."

Silas snorts and looks back at me. I want to punch him in his face. The man is practically gloating.

"Well, it is hard to believe, but I guess I just felt sorry for him. Call it charity work," Silas says as he releases her hand.

Leah giggles. When she meets my gaze, her smile falls, and she looks like a Little girl who just got in trouble. I suppose I did scold her like a Little girl for climbing on the roof. She needed to be scolded. What if I hadn't come home? What if she'd fallen? There were so many things that could have gone wrong. If she were mine, she'd have a red-hot bottom right now and would be writing lines about safety. Then she'd be getting a second spanking at bedtime as another reminder.

But she's not mine. And I'm an asshole for even thinking thoughts like that.

"I'm going to put some fans in your room to start drying it out," I say, a bit gruffer than I'd planned.

She nods, then her eyes go comically wide, and she practically darts off my porch toward me. "Wait! I can put the fans in there."

Jaxon

I grab hold of her biceps when she tries to pass me. She's panicking. She knows if I go into her room that I'll discover who she is. Too bad I already know.

"Leah, I saw. It's fine," I say quietly.

The last thing I want is to draw Silas' attention to her bedroom, but I also don't want to embarrass her more than she already is. Her cheeks are turning bright red as her eyes dart everywhere.

"It's fine," I say again. "Please go inside where it's warm while I get the fans going."

"But..."

"Leah," I growl.

Her shoulders drop, and she gives me a slight bob of her head before she turns to go back to my house.

"I'll see you in the morning," I say to Silas.

The grin he's sporting is pissing me off, but he seems to realize I'm in no mood for his shit tonight because he just winks. "Sure thing, *boss*. It was nice meeting you, Leah. Maybe I'll see you around some time."

Leah gives him a wide smile. "Maybe."

Yeah, that's not happening.

As soon as my so-called friend is gone and Leah is back inside, I grab the fans and take them into her room. With the amount of water that's dripped onto her bed, I'm worried she might have to replace everything. Between the fans and turning the heat up, though, maybe she'll luck out.

When I finally get back to my house, my heart starts to hammer in my chest at the sight of her. She's sitting on the floor in my kitchen with her back against the cabinet, a mug of tea in her hand, and my dog sprawled across her legs. And she's crying. Fuck. Me.

Unsure of what to do, I clear my throat. She gasps and runs the back of her hand over her cheeks before she looks up at me.

"Why are you sitting on the floor in the kitchen?" I ask.

She sniffles, and it feels like my heart is being ripped out. I hate it when women cry. I never know what to do. It's one thing when they're in Little Space and they're crying because I just spanked their bottom, but when they're just plain sad, it kills me.

"I didn't want to get your couch wet."

Jesus. So instead, she's freezing her little butt off on my tile floor. I lower my hand in front of her face. "Come on. Up."

She stares blankly at my fingers for several seconds before she takes them and lets me help her up.

"You're going to need to sleep in another room for a few days while the fans are running. You should also keep the heat turned up to help it dry out. When the rain stops, I'll take a closer look at your roof and see what needs to be done."

When she lets out a long, low sigh, I want to pull her to my chest and reassure her that everything will be okay. I don't even know this woman, but I'm pretty sure she's been through some shit in her life lately, and right now, it's a bit too much for her to handle. The dark circles under her eyes make me want to pick her up, carry her to my bed, and tuck her in for a few days of rest.

"Right. Well, thank you for your help. I'll look into finding a roofer. I'm pretty sure the whole thing needs to be replaced. I just hadn't thought it would need to be done so soon," she says before she plasters on a smile that I know is forced. "Guess that's all part of buying a house, right? Anyway, thanks again."

Oh, no. She isn't getting away that easily. She was just crying on my kitchen floor a moment ago, and now she's pretending to be all bubbly. I might be dense sometimes, but I'm not blind.

I rest my hand on her shoulder. At least this way I can

Jaxon

hold her at a safe distance so I don't pull her against my body.

"Do not get on your roof again, Leah. Do you understand me? It isn't safe."

A flash of defiance sparkles in her eyes but disappears quickly. "Jaxon, I can take care of myself. I don't need your permission to get up on *my* roof. I appreciate your help today, but I can handle it from here."

Something that feels like indigestion settles in my chest. She's not going to make this easy for me. Of course, why would she? I'm no one to her. Just a grouchy neighbor.

"Give me your phone," I snap.

"What?"

I sigh and hold out my hand. "Give me your phone. I'm going to put my number in it. If you have any other leaks happen between now and when it dries, call me. Don't. Climb. On. The. Roof. Are we clear?"

I'm being a jerk and I know it, but I mean well and that counts for something, right?

5

LEAH

I am utterly humiliated. I want to fall into a sinkhole and never be found again. This has been a terrible day, and all I wanted was to come home, eat some childish snacks, and spend the evening enjoying Little Space. But noooo. Instead, I have a rainforest in my house, my neighbor knows I'm a Little, I have to replace my whole damn roof, and I'm so incredibly tired, I can barely stand up straight. And on top of all that, he's trying to tell me what I can and can't do.

What I *should* do is tell him off, then set him straight on life and how he doesn't get to boss me around. But instead, I find myself handing over my phone. When he holds it up to my face to unlock it, I roll my eyes. He's maddening. And way too hot for his own good. A man this crotchety shouldn't be this dang fine. It's irritating.

His phone dings before he hands mine back to me. "Here. I sent myself a message so I have your number too. I'll get in touch with you after I figure out what the verdict is on your roof. But until then, if you have any other leaks, call or text me, Leah. Day or night, I don't care. Just don't get on that roof again."

He's really starting to get on my nerves with all his demands.

"Why is it okay for you to get on my roof, but not me?" I demand, popping a hand on my hip.

His perma-scowl shifts into a slightly amused one as he stares down at me. "Because I have experience and I know what to look for. I don't suppose you've climbed on many roofs over the years?"

My Little side wants to kick him in the shins for being such a know-it-all, but my traitorous vagina is swooning at his show of dominance. It's all very confusing.

"Well, no. But—"

"But nothing, Leah. Just let me take care of this. I'll sleep better at night if you promise not to get up there again."

I roll my eyes and scoff. "Because I live to help you sleep better at night."

"Little girl," he says in a low voice.

Ugh. Poop. I'd hoped maybe he hadn't noticed all the stuff in my bedroom when he'd gone in there. Or if he had, he didn't realize what it all meant.

I shuffle my feet, unable to look up at him. I don't want to see his judgment. I saw enough of that from my ex.

"Yeah, okay. I won't go up there again," I say quietly as I make my way toward the front door.

Before I reach it, Jaxon grabs my wrist. The warmth of his other hand caresses my chin as he forces my head back. His face is firmly set, and he's clenching his jaw.

"Don't ever be ashamed of who or what you are, Leah. Whoever made you feel embarrassed of it is an asshole. There's nothing wrong with being Little."

My eyes burn with tears. How was he able to read me so easily? Why does he even care?

"My ex-wife made me feel ashamed of being a Daddy, so I know what it feels like. Don't fall for that bullshit. You're perfect just as you are. Okay?" he adds.

Jaxon

I blink several times, trying to make the tears go away before I start crying in front of this confusing man. He's a jerk. A total grouch. Way too bossy. But he understands. And he just admitted to being a Daddy. My heart is racing at that little piece of information, and my pussy is practically doing somersaults. He's probably a good Daddy. Despite his terrible personality issues.

The look in his eyes is almost tender, and I kind of want to lean into his touch. But I'm pretty sure the man hates me, and I'm not looking for a relationship anyway, so I need to get the hell out of here before I do something else to embarrass myself.

"Okay. Thank you. I'll text you if any other leaks appear."

He drops his hands and swallows. His Adam's apple bobs in his thick neck, and my nipples tighten. I need to go. Like five minutes ago.

Willie bumps his nose on my leg, and I smile. This dog has already won my heart. I lean down and give the furball a kiss on his head. "Bye, one-eyed Willie."

Jaxon groans. I giggle at the sound.

"His new name is Dog. At least until I figure out something else."

My eyebrows shoot up. "You can't rename him now. You'll confuse him. Willie is a perfectly adorable name."

He rolls his eyes, and the corner of his mouth is twitching like he almost wants to smile. He doesn't, though, of course. God forbid he bless the world with something like that.

With one last pat on Willie's head, I open the front door and make my way back toward my house. I have several hours of clean up to do before bed. I just hope I can save all my stuffies. My bed and blankets are replaceable, but my stuffies are my best friends. At least I have plenty of things to think about while I clean up because I have a feeling Jaxon is going to be running through my mind like a marathon.

Two hours later, the bedroom that I spent two straight days unpacking and making just perfect is now in shambles. I've stripped the bed and started running the sheets through the laundry. My stuffed animals are still in a pile away from the drip and for some reason, I'm terrified to start cleaning them up because I'll be devastated if any of them are ruined. I've had most of them for at least twenty years.

The industrial fans Jaxon set up in my room are excessively loud. The ceiling is no longer dripping, so that's a plus.

I'm about to tackle my pile of stuffed animals when my phone alerts me of a text message. When I look at the screen and see Jaxon's name, I feel a little flutter low in my tummy. It's dumb considering he's probably only texting me to talk about my roof. I really need to get my bodily reactions to him in check.

> Jaxon: I found this information online about the best way to dry stuffed animals without ruining them.

A slow smile spreads across my face as I click on the link he sent. He researched how to save my toys? I shouldn't be feeling all gooey and fluttery inside over this, but I totally am. The big jerk maybe isn't such a big jerk after all.

> Leah: I don't know what to say.

> Jaxon: Most people would just say thank you.

Okay, he *is* a big jerk. A big, grouchy, obnoxious jerk and again, I find myself thinking about wanting to kick him in the shins. Right after I hug him for being so thoughtful.

Kevin would have told me to throw all of them out. He wouldn't have even thought twice. Then again, he hated all my toys. They were just a reminder of what I couldn't give him because my body is broken.

I push all those thoughts away and focus on my phone.

> Leah: Thank you. It means a lot to me.

> Jaxon: You're welcome.

Maybe the man doesn't hate me. Maybe we can be neighborly toward each other. Like normal people who don't know each other's secret interests. Yeah, right. I will never get the thought of Jaxon being a Daddy out of my head. Even though it's hard to picture the big grumpy guy being a tender and caring Daddy, somehow I know he probably is. He's probably a great Daddy. I'll bet he's super strict.

A shiver runs through me. Being spanked by Jaxon would be…hot. And maybe a little terrifying. The man has huge hands. Not to mention he's enormous, and he looks incredibly strong. He'd probably be able to manhandle even someone like me. Not that he would want to. He could have his pick of women. He certainly isn't going to want to play with me. Not a chance in hell. Not that I would want to play with him anyway. I mean, my pussy wants to. That needy bitch has been catcalling him for days, but it can't happen for so many reasons.

6

JAXON

It's been two days since I covered Leah's roof with tarps. Other than the short text conversation we had about the best way to dry her toys, I haven't heard from her. I'm hoping that and the fact that I haven't seen her on her roof since then means she hasn't had any more leaks.

The rain is still coming down, which means I haven't had a chance to get on top of her house yet. The shape the roof is in worries me. The woman that lives under that roof worries me too.

I can't forget the look on her face when I called her Little girl. It was pure shame and embarrassment. Someone made her feel like being Little was a bad thing. Whoever it was, I'd like to have words with them and set them straight. I hope what I said to her made her feel better. When I sent her the information about how to dry her toys without ruining them, I was hoping she would understand that I'm not a threat to her Little side. Hell, I feel even more protective over her now knowing what she is.

I've been worrying about where she's been sleeping since she can't sleep in her bedroom. Is she getting enough rest, or does she still have those dark circles under her eyes? Has she been able to regress the past couple of days? So many things I want to know and can't seem to stop thinking about but wish I could. I really need to make a trip to Twisted. I need to have sex and Daddy someone for a night. It would be a reset button. Maybe if I do that, I'll stop thinking about the Little girl next door.

The number of times I've picked up my phone the past couple of days, wanting to text her and find out how the drying process is going—and how she's doing—is embarrassing. I've never wanted to text a woman so badly and it's pissing me off. I don't even know Leah. I'm not interested in getting involved with anyone. Wendy ruined relationships for me.

Willie unfolds himself from the ball he's curled up in and trots to the back door. Just another Saturday night at home. Austin asked if I wanted to go get some beers at The Tap Room, the one and only bar in Pine Hollow, but I turned him down. I swear I'm still feeling the effects of my hangover from last weekend. Damn, I'm getting old.

When I open the back door to let the dog, who I'm still considering renaming, out, the rain has let up some. Willie does his business while I stand in the doorway. I happen to look over at Leah's backyard. In Pine Hollow, most lots are separated by short picket fencing. Apparently, people around here don't like privacy fences. I considered putting one up shortly after I moved in, but at the time, my direct neighbors never bothered me, so I didn't really see the point. I should probably reconsider it.

All I can think about as I look over at her yard is the fact that I'll be able to watch Leah while she plays. That is, *if* she plays back there. I know she works as a florist at Blossom and Bloom, so maybe she'll be the type to go plant a bunch of flowers while getting filthy in the dirt. I wouldn't mind helping her clean up afterward. Fuck. I need to keep my distance. She's getting under my skin, and I've only talked to her twice.

Since Willie seems to be taking his sweet time finding the perfect spot to poop, I leave the back door open and pull the steak I'm planning to have for dinner out of the fridge. Suddenly, a loud siren sounds in the distance. I jump at the sound. It takes a few seconds to realize it's a smoke detector, and it's coming from Leah's house.

I dart out back and see smoke coming out of her open sliding glass door. Without a second thought, I hop the fence and run inside. That was a big fucking mistake on my part.

"Leah! Fuck!"

She's standing on the damn counter in her kitchen waving a towel near the smoke detector. I swear I'm having heart palpitations again. Not just because she's on the counter but because of what she's wearing. An oversized knit sweater with a bear embroidered on the front and a pair of pastel striped thigh high socks. And to top it all off, she's stretching to try to reach the smoke detector, and her sweater is high enough I can see her panties. They look like a pair of training panties. Full cut with padding in the crotch. Her hair is in pigtails with matching bows clipped in at the base of each one. Fuck. Me.

"Gah! Jaxon! You scared me!" she squeals.

I rush to her and put my hands on her hips to lift her off the counter. When she's back on the ground, I take the towel from her and fan the smoke detector until it finally shuts off.

It takes me several seconds of counting in my head before I can face her. Right now, I want to put her over my lap and spank some sense into her but if she's in Little Space, which I suspect she is, I don't want to scare her.

Finally, I turn around and pin her with a firm stare. "Little girl. What is it with you and climbing on things? Do you want to give me a heart attack?"

She doesn't look scared. Instead, she looks like an

adorable Little girl who just got caught climbing on the counter by her Daddy. And fuck, I wish I was that Daddy.

When she doesn't answer me, I tilt my head. "Answer me, Little bear."

"I was making dinner and I started watching a movie and forgot it was in the oven," she says quietly.

She's twisting her fingers together nervously, and she has her bottom lip captured between her teeth. She's the cutest Little girl I've ever laid eyes on.

I let out a deep sigh. She's in Little Space. She shouldn't be making her own dinner. I glance at the pan on the counter that has two burnt-to-a-crisp chicken nuggets that look like coals and seven French fries on it.

"That's your dinner?" I ask, a little more harshly than I intended.

"Errr…um…well, yeah."

"Leah, that's not even a fucking snack. Why are you only having two chicken nuggets and seven French fries for dinner?"

She twists her fingers together some more, and I'm relieved that her sweater is now covering her panties, but I wish it covered her luscious thighs too. I could kiss and bite that soft flesh all damn night.

"Because it's a half a portion and I'm trying to eat less," she says quietly.

I narrow my eyes and roughly cup her chin between my fingers, forcing her to look at me. I'm finding it very hard not to lose my shit right now.

"Why are you trying to eat less? For what purpose?" I demand.

Even though I still have hold of her chin, her eyes dart around the room nervously. "Because I'm fat, and I need to lose weight. But I really wanted chicken nuggets and fries, so I thought having a half portion would be good enough."

Every cell in my body freezes, and I'm barely hanging on by a thread. Someone hurt her, and I want to kill them for it.

"Look at me. You are *perfect*. You're healthy and beautiful and precious just the way you are. Do you know how many men would drop to their fucking knees over how perfect you are?"

Her bottom lip trembles.

"Two chicken nuggets isn't acceptable. Hell, four chicken nuggets isn't even an acceptable portion size. Jesus. Who the fuck told you that you need to lose weight? I want their name and number right now."

Her eyes widen. "What? Jaxon, don't be ridiculous."

I release her chin and wave at the baking sheet. "This is fucking ridiculous. The fact that you think you need to lose weight and that you're not even eating a snack size portion for dinner is ridiculous. Not acceptable, Little bear. You need nutrients and protein and calories."

She looks so ashamed it breaks my heart. If only she could see what I see when I look at her, she would have no insecurities about the way she looks. The woman is runway gorgeous. She's probably considered plus size, but fuck, that's beautiful. More plus-size women need to be on the runway if you ask me. What man wouldn't want to worship a set of thick thighs that jiggle when you're pounding into her? The thought of Leah's thighs wrapped around me makes my cock thicken in my jeans.

I force those thoughts away because right now, I have a Little girl who feels sad and ashamed standing in front of me. She was trying to have a fun night spent in Little Space and I'll be damned if that doesn't happen.

"I'll tell you what. You go watch your movie, and I'll make your dinner. Little girls shouldn't be touching the oven anyway."

7

LEAH

Did I just hear him right? Am I going deaf? Am I hallucinating? Because surely my hot Daddy neighbor didn't just offer to make me dinner. And why is it that every time I see him, I'm always humiliated? First the bear onesie, then my room, now I'm completely submerged in Little Space, outfit and all, and here he is. My enormous thighs are on display, I'm not wearing any pants, and I'm pretty sure he saw my training panties. I wouldn't normally wish for something else to go wrong with my house, but I wouldn't mind if a sinkhole opened up in my floor and sucked me down.

"Little bear," he says in that stern voice that has my eyes snapping up to his.

"What?"

What had he said? I don't remember now. I was too busy overthinking everything to death.

He sighs, and I think he's fighting a smile again. I really want to see him smile. It's probably earth shatteringly hot. He puts his hands on my shoulders and spins me around toward the living room where I have a makeshift fort set up, then nudges me forward.

"Go watch your movie. I got dinner. And you're eating more than two damn chicken nuggets."

My Little side is swooning. An utter pile of goo. This man is offering to make me dinner because apparently my Little side doesn't know how to cook very well. My adult side, which is peeking out just slightly, is panicking and wants to push this big ogre out of my house.

I turn around to look at him again. "You don't have to. I'm sure you have better things to do tonight."

"I don't. I was just going to hang out with my dog and watch TV. Now, quit stalling and get back to your movie."

With a hesitant sigh, I turn around, then pause and look back at him. "Thank you."

It comes out as a whisper, but he hears it, and his stern expression softens.

"You're welcome, Little bear."

I smile at him. A genuine smile because his kindness is really touching. Maybe my first impression of him wasn't the best. Maybe there's something more behind that gruff exterior. Actually, I'm sure there is because his dog looks at him like he hung the moon and that tells me enough to know that Jaxon Sawyer is probably a decent man.

"Can Willie come over?" I ask.

He smiles. An actual smile. It makes the corners of his eyes crinkle and I get a glimpse of his pearly white teeth. And I was right, it is earth shattering.

Jaxon disappears out of the back slider and, a few seconds later, reappears with an excited Willie at his side. As soon as the dog sees me, his tail swishes wildly as he runs toward me. I giggle and lower myself to the floor to pet him.

"Hi, buddy. I missed you."

Willie responds with a lick to my entire face. I squeal and giggle. A low chuckle makes me freeze. Did Jaxon just laugh? Oh my God! That was a sexy sound. Okay, I need to chill. Note to self: Don't think about his laugh.

Jaxon

When I'm back on my feet, I hesitate. "Do you want help?"

Jaxon's eyes narrow, and he clenches his jaw. "Go watch your movie. I got this."

Sheesh. Back to being bossy. With a sigh, I make my way to the living room and plop down on the couch. Only a few seconds after pressing play on my movie, it pauses, and I realize Jaxon is standing beside the couch with the remote in hand. And he's glaring at me.

"When you burned your chicken nuggets, were you sitting on the couch watching your movie or were you in your fort?"

I pull my bottom lip between my teeth. Why? Why does he always have to ask me things? Will he judge me if I tell him the truth?

"Do. Not. Think. About. Lying. To. Me," he adds.

Shoot.

"I was in the fort."

He grabs hold of my wrist. With a gentle tug, he pulls me up from the couch and nudges me toward the opening of the fort.

"Don't change what you were doing for me. If you like watching movies in your fort, I want you to do that. You were spending the evening in Little Space, you're supposed to enjoy it. I'm a Daddy, Leah. I want you to enjoy this and I don't want you to hold back because I'm here. Just be you."

I look back at him, completely flustered. What do I even say to that? He wants me to be me. That's not something I'm used to. But when he gives me another nudge, I drop to my knees and crawl into my magical fort with Willie right alongside me.

Jaxon lets out a grunt, and I remember I don't have pants on and I just crawled in front of him. Shoot. I really am going to die of embarrassment. I'm never coming out of this fort. Nope. Not happening. Jaxon Sawyer just saw my big fat butt and all the dimples that come along with it.

When I hear him moving around in the kitchen, I settle against the pillows and watch the movie that he started again. Willie lets out a sigh and curls up next to me. If I weren't so horrified, I'd be having the time of my life right now.

"Little bear."

I pop my head out of the fort and find Jaxon with a plate in his hand. He kneels, and his eyes roam the magical space I've created. Using some of my moving boxes, I draped an enormous quilt over them to create a ceiling, then used smaller blankets for the walls. After that, I strung up some battery-operated twinkle lights and added a bunch of throw pillows and blankets to the mix. I have a few stuffies in here, including Buttercup, that are all dry, and I've spent the past two nights sleeping in this special little space I created.

"You did a good job on your fort," he says.

I smile up at him, thrilled by his praise.

He holds a plate out in front of me. "Dinner. Do you have a cup in here or should I find one in the cupboard?"

My cheeks heat because I do have a cup already but it's a sippy cup. As though he can read my mind, he holds his free hand out. "Give me your cup."

Slowly, I offer it to him. Without hesitation, he takes hold of one of the handles, his hand dwarfing the thing completely.

"Milk or water?"

I give him my sweetest smile. "Juice?"

His entire face relaxes as he chuckles. "Nice try. With dinner, you can have milk or water."

Jaxon

Rude. Who made him the boss? But also, my princess parts are totally going wild over him sort of Daddying me.

"Water, please."

He winks. "Good girl using your manners. Start eating."

A moment later when he comes back, he kneels again and hands me my cup. When he goes to rise, I reach out and touch his forearm. His very muscular forearm I might add. He pauses to look at me.

"Thank you for being so nice. It's been a rough week, and I needed this tonight. I didn't expect you to be here, but it's made my night better."

He swallows, his dark brown eyes searching my face for several seconds before he lets out a quiet grunt. Is it weird that I'm starting to find his grunts endearing?

"You can..." Oh, my gosh, I'm an idiot. Why was I just about to invite him to stay? Like he would actually want to.

"What?"

I shake my head. "Nothing."

"Little bear," he growls. "Use your words. What were you going to say?"

"I was going to say you can stay and watch the movie with me if you want, but then I realized that was a stupid thing to say."

When his brows furrow and his eyes narrow, a shiver runs through me. He didn't like that answer. Nope, not one bit.

"Your eye is twitching," I murmur.

Crumb. Shut up, Leah.

"I don't know what kind of people you've had in your life who made you doubt yourself, but I really want to kick their asses. It wasn't a stupid thing to ask. I'd love to watch the movie. I'm just going to grab a beer from my house. I'll be right back. Scoot over and make room because I'm nowhere near as tiny as you."

A flush warms my cheeks. While I'm not even close to

being tiny, I do feel extra Little around him, which is a nice feeling for once. I start scooting over as he stands.

"And get to eating your dinner, Little girl," he calls out before he opens my sliding glass door.

Mr. Bossy is back, and I am totally here for it. Thank goodness for training panties because my regular panties would already be soaked through by now.

I quickly grab one of the throw blankets I have in the fort and cover myself so he doesn't get another glimpse of my fat thighs. Maybe I should go put on a pair of pants. Before I can scurry out, Jaxon returns and somehow folds himself in a way that he's able to get into my magical fort without causing it to collapse. Having him this close to me is a really bad idea because the man smells edible.

"We can watch a different movie if you want," I offer.

He frowns at me. I'm surprised the man doesn't have more wrinkles with as much as he frowns.

"I happen to love *Monsters Inc*, so press play and, for the love of all things holy, eat your dinner."

Before I can say anything, he picks up a chicken nugget and holds it to my mouth. "Bite."

I'm blushing like crazy as I try to take the nugget from his fingers. He pulls his hand away.

"Little girls who don't eat when they're told get hand fed," he grumbles.

Even though he's acting grouchy, his eyes tell me he might actually be enjoying himself, so I open my mouth and accept the bite he's offering. I don't know if I'll ever have another Daddy, so I might as well enjoy this one night of having my overprotective, bossy, ridiculously sexy neighbor Daddying me. It will be a night that I will no doubt remember for the rest of my life. And every time I use my vibrator.

8

JAXON

Her blond pigtails swish every time she moves, and I have filthy thoughts in my head about grabbing hold of them to guide her mouth to my cock. This Little girl is testing my willpower. My brain knows I can't get involved with her. My cock, on the other hand...he has other ideas.

Just feeding her chicken nuggets is turning into this erotic thing that's making me painfully hard.

"Can I give Willie a chicky nugget?" she asks while she strokes my dog's head.

I wish she were stroking other things. Fuck. I'm an asshole.

"I want you to eat your chicken nuggets. Willie already had dinner."

She pops her bottom lip out in a pout. I raise an eyebrow and give her a stern look as I hold a nugget up to her lips.

"No pouting. Bite."

She obeys, and fuck if that doesn't make me proud. Her mix of sassy and sweet is intoxicating. Although I do wish I could swat her bottom when she sasses me, but I'll visit that fantasy in my mind later tonight in the shower.

After seven nuggets and a handful of French fries, she rubs her tummy. "I'm full."

"Are you really full or are you just saying that because you think you should stop?"

When she looks at me, I can tell she's being honest. She's so easy to read, which is somewhat of an advantage for me.

"I really am full. Thank you."

I set the plate aside and lean back against all the throw pillows she's added to her little fort. We finish watching the movie. I'm painfully hard the entire time from being so close to her. I need to go home. Get some space and air.

"Have you been sleeping in here?" I ask when I notice her pacifier and a few stuffies off to the side.

She glances at me nervously. "Yeah, but I think my room is almost dry."

"The rain is supposed to clear up tomorrow. I'll get on the roof and check it out. Mind if I go test the ceiling in your room to make sure it's solid?"

"Okay."

Crawling in and out of her fort is a test in agility for me. I think I've pulled three muscles just folding and unfolding myself. When did I become an old man?

As I make my way to her bedroom, Leah giggles at something that's on TV and it makes me feel warm all over. She has one of those laughs that's soft and sweet and makes everyone around her smile because it's that damn contagious. Being here is making me have thoughts that I have no business thinking.

Once I've confirmed her ceiling isn't going to cave in, I return to the living room and squat down at the opening of her fort. "Your ceiling is solid. Thankfully the water was leaking from the opening of the light fixture instead of pooling on the drywall. It feels pretty dry. Give the fans another night before you set your bedroom back up. I'll stop

Jaxon

by tomorrow and get up on the roof to check things out. It's supposed to be dry for the next couple of days."

The pink hue of her cheeks—and the way she's nibbling on her bottom lip—is testing my ability to think straight. Her wide eyes are so innocent. I hate that she lives in this house by herself. It's not my problem, though. She isn't my girl and where she lives is none of my business. At least that's what I'm going to keep telling myself.

"Thank you. You didn't have to do all this."

Yeah, I did. But instead of saying that, I smile and feed her some bullshit. "Yeah, but we're neighbors and neighbors help each other out. Right?"

God, even *I* don't believe that. I haven't helped a single person on this entire block since I moved in. Maybe I'm becoming a better man. Or maybe I'm a perverted asshole and the only organ I'm thinking with is my dick.

"Right," she says slowly.

"I'm going to get going." I have to leave. If I don't get out of here, I'll do something I might regret. I don't miss the look of disappointment flitting across her features, but she quickly masks it. Fuck.

"Okay," she says as she starts crawling out of the fort.

I head for her sliding glass door. "Come on, dog."

She giggles but doesn't say anything about my new name choice for Willie.

"Thanks for, uh, coming. It was really nice of you." Her eyes are cast down and she's shifting from foot to foot like a nervous Little girl. She's so fucking genuine. It's refreshing. My ex-wife wouldn't have understood the word genuine if the definition was tattooed on her forehead.

When I don't say anything for a long time, she finally looks up at me.

"Good girl. I like seeing your eyes."

The pink tinge on her cheeks deepens, and she twists her

legs together, almost dancing. Does she need the potty? Fuck. No. She's squeezing her thighs together. Like she *wants* me. Because I called her a good girl? I'm pretty sure she hasn't had enough praise in her life based on how negatively she talks about herself. It's amazing how some people thrive off a little positive encouragement. Leah is one of those people.

Pinning her with a stern look, I take a step closer, and she lets out a quiet gasp.

"No more climbing on stuff. If you need to reach something, call me. Do not do it yourself. Got it?"

If I wasn't so damn serious about this issue, I might think the little eyeroll she's giving me was cute. But instead, I want to bend her over the dining room table and smack her round bottom until she understands just how serious I am.

"Leah," I say in warning.

The corners of her mouth curl up in a smile. "Okay. Got it. Call my giant neighbor to reach high things."

"*Leah.*"

She laughs and rolls her eyes again. "I got it, big guy. No more climbing. Now go and take your one-eyed Willie home so I can watch another movie."

I grumble under my breath and shake my head as I step outside. "You're a brat."

Leah pats Willie's head and beams up at me. "Only sometimes. It usually happens when my big bossy neighbor is around, being all big and bossy and stuff. Normally I'm quite sweet."

My cock twitches. Yeah, I'll bet she's sweet. Her pussy probably tastes like honey. Damn, I wouldn't mind being Winnie the Pooh for a night so I could get into that honey pot.

I grunt in response and force myself to walk away. "Goodnight, Leah."

"Night, Jaxon. Night, Willie-boy."

Jaxon

I'm not in the mood for my steak, so I grab a beer instead and head to my ensuite bathroom. There's only one thing I want right now and that's the Little girl that lives next door. And since I can't have her, I'll settle for the next best thing. A shower beer and masturbation.

9

LEAH

When I wake up in my awesome little fort, my mind automatically travels to last night. Jaxon. In my house. Seeing me in my training panties and thigh-high socks. All while I was so deeply in Little Space that I let him take care of me. He made me dinner. And filled my sippy cup. He even climbed into my fort, which is way too small for a big guy like him. It's a night I'll never forget. Hell, in the two hours he spent with me, he was a better caregiver than my ex had ever been. Kind of makes me wonder what I ever saw in Kevin.

Well, I know what I saw in him. He was smooth talking. A charmer. He knew how to flap his lips to get what he wanted. I find it interesting that Jaxon is his complete opposite. The man was as charming as a grizzly bear, yet the prize is under his rough exterior.

I finally crawl out of my little nest of blankets—because my bladder is about to explode—I make my way to the bathroom. Since it's Sunday, I need to make good use of my time and try to get my house somewhat in order. I've emptied most of the moving boxes, and my counters are no longer littered with things I don't know what to do with. If I'm productive all day, my place might actually resemble a cozy home by this evening. I'm excited to put my bedroom back together. As much fun as it's been sleeping in my fort, the floor isn't nearly as comfortable as my bed.

Reluctantly, I change out of my Little pajamas and pull out my pigtails, replacing them with black leggings and a messy bun on top of my head. After making myself a cup of coffee, I load the dishwasher and start it. It only takes a few minutes to disassemble all the blankets and make the living room look more put together.

In need of another cup of coffee, I head to the kitchen and come to an abrupt stop, my eyes practically bulging. Water gushing from under my dishwasher. I panic and yank the door open to stop it before I run to the bathroom to gather towels. This is not how my Sunday is supposed to go. I just need one day where I don't have to handle anything major in this house. All I wanted to do was clean today. Make it nice and cozy and light a candle. Relax and read a book about a hot Daddy I'll never actually get to have. But noooo. Of course something has to go wrong. I'm starting to think this house is cursed.

I grab my phone and start searching for videos to help me figure out what could be wrong. I can't afford a new dishwasher right now. Especially since I'm pretty sure I'm going to be replacing my entire roof. After nearly forty-five minutes of searching, I'm pretty sure I've found the problem. It should be a simple fix. Once I get back from the hardware store, that is. I really do need to ask about a frequent buyer program.

Without grabbing a second cup of coffee, I head out to my car and drive the short distance to The Rusty Screw. The name of the store makes me smile. Most of the places in this town have somewhat odd but cute names. Like The Pepperoni Palace Pizzeria. Or Sugar and Sprinkles Bakery. Or Java Junkies. Even the florist shop where I work.

Jaxon

Blossom and Bloom. Who thinks of this stuff? I guess it's one of those things people love about towns like this. Everything is quaint and cozy and everyone is friendly.

As soon as I walk into the hardware store, a woman behind the counter greets me. I've seen her here before, but she's always been with other customers. Even though we've never spoken, I'm drawn to her. Maybe it's because every time I've seen her, she's had pigtails in her hair or space buns or braids and she always has ribbons or bows attached. None of that means she's a Little but my wishful side hopes I won't be the only Little in Pine Hollow. It would be so nice to find some like-minded friends. I haven't had that in so long.

"Good morning. What can I help you with?" She's so bubbly as she speaks and her smile lights up her whole face. I have a feeling she's a total glass half full kind of girl.

I tell her the name of the part I need, and she points down an aisle. When I make my way in that direction, she comes around the counter and follows me.

"You're new around here, right? I've seen you in here a couple of times, but I haven't caught your name. I'm Natalie."

I pause my search and turn to her with a smile. The woman looks around my age. She's plus size like me, but I'm jealous of her curves. She has a beautiful shape. Unlike me. As she holds her hand out to shake mine, she's bouncing on her toes. I like this girl.

"Nice to meet you. I'm Leah. And yeah. I'm new here. I just moved to Pine Hollow a couple of weeks ago."

Natalie's face lights up. "That's so awesome! What moved you out here? I mean, don't get me wrong, Pine Hollow is charming, but it's also a tiny town. Most people try to escape towns like this."

"I, uh, I went through a divorce. I hated living in Portland. I've always wanted to live in a small town like this. I drove through here one time years ago and fell in love. When

I decided to move away, I reached out to Blossom and Bloom to see if they were looking for a florist and they were, so it made the decision easy. So, here I am."

Natalie's face morphs into understanding. "I just went through a divorce myself. Unfortunately, he still lives in this town. I avoid him like the plague, though. Anyways. We should hang out sometime. We're both newly divorced. I can introduce you to some other women here in town if you want to make some friends?"

She talks so fast that it takes me a second to catch up but, when I do, my chest warms at her invitation. This is exactly why I wanted to move to a small town. People tend to be more welcoming. At least that's what it seems so far.

"I'd like that, actually," I say with a smile.

She beams at me before her eyes flick to my purse. "Oh my gosh, I love your bunny keychain. Bunnies are my favorite. I have one named Cotton Ball."

My cheeks warm as I look down at the small fluffy keychain. It's attached to the outside of my purse so whenever I feel anxious, I can run my fingers through the fur. Most people don't notice it. Hopefully Natalie doesn't think I'm weird.

"Cool. I love rabbits. And all animals. Well, only if they have fur. Except furry spiders. Those are terrifying. How many bunnies do you have?"

Shoot. I'm totally rambling, and I want to grab Thumper and run my fingers through his fur, but I also don't want to draw more attention to my toy.

Natalie giggles and pulls out her phone. "Cotton Ball is my stuffie. I don't have any real rabbits. See. He's the one in the front."

She turns her phone to show me a picture of a pile of stuffed animals. Right in the front is a long-haired stuffed bunny. There are other toys mixed into the pile and my eyes widen.

"Are you…"

Natalie leans closer to me and grins. "I'm a Little. I suspect you are too."

I stare at her with my mouth hanging open. When I finally get myself together, I bite my bottom lip, trying not to smile too wide. "I am. How did you know?"

She shrugs. "Kindred spirits and all that jazz, maybe? Or it could be that I've seen you in here several times, and you've had pigtails in your hair, or a cute, animated shirt on, or a stuffed bunny hanging off your purse. I was pretty sure you were a Little even if you didn't already know it."

I burst out giggling, using my hand to cover my mouth. "Oh my gosh. I can't believe you could tell. I need to hide myself better."

Her expression turns serious as she furrows her eyebrows. "Why would you ever want to hide yourself? You're perfect just as you are, and the people here will love you no matter what. Besides, there are a lot more Littles and Daddies in this town than you'd expect."

A face I recognize comes into view, and Natalie turns.

"Speaking of," she mumbles.

"Natalie," he says coolly, his expression searching before he turns to me. "Leah. Nice to see you again."

I smile at Silas. "Nice to see you again too."

Natalie blushes and scurries away, murmuring something about going to check on merchandise in the back. Silas watches her, and I don't miss the way his eyes linger on her backside before he turns his attention back to me. I smirk at him, but he ignores it.

"What are you doing here on this fine Sunday?" he asks, motioning toward the row of dishwasher parts.

"Oh, my dishwasher is on the fritz. I think it's just a gasket," I reply as I turn to look at the display.

"You ask Jaxon to look at it? He's good at that kind of stuff."

I narrow my eyes at him. "I'm capable of doing it."

Silas holds up his hands like he's surrendering, but the corner of his mouth is tipped up. "Sorry I asked. I'm sure you're more than capable."

It takes great restraint not to stick my tongue out at the man. His friend might know I'm a Little but that doesn't mean I want the entire town knowing. However, I do wonder if Silas knows that Jaxon is a Daddy. Hmm. Interesting thought. Maybe Silas is a Daddy too. I glance at him, but my body doesn't react the way it does for my surly neighbor. That's too bad. Silas is a little smoother around the edges than Jaxon. Then again, he was also just checking out Natalie's butt. Makes me wonder if there's something between them. Not that it's my business. Look at me being all small town gossip-like. Making something out of nothing.

I quickly grab what I need and head up to the cash register where I exchange phone numbers with Natalie. I give Silas a friendly smile as I leave. "See you later, Silas."

He gives me a full-wattage grin and winks. "You too. Good luck with your dishwasher."

Hmph. I don't need luck. I have YouTube. And common sense.

Do not cry, Leah. Do not freaking cry.

I'm going to cry. I spent the last hour and a half changing out this stupid gasket and felt like I was on top of the world when I restarted my dishwasher. Only as I stood there with a grin on my face, giving myself a mental pat on the back, water started seeping out of the bottom again. A lot of water. I had to run back to the bathroom and find more towels to sop up this new pool in my kitchen.

I lower myself to the tile floor and sit criss-cross applesauce while I look up more videos on YouTube. As much as I want to be able to do all of this, I'm in over my head right now and it's times like this I really wish I had someone to lean on.

After watching five new videos, I think it might be a hose that's broken, which makes sense since the water is coming from underneath the dishwasher. Even though I'm a sweaty wreck at this point, I need to make another trip to the hardware store. Hopefully Natalie won't judge me for my appearance. I just don't have the energy to fix myself. I'm barely hanging on by a thread.

I swing my front door open and collide with a wide, solid chest. It knocks me off balance but before I tumble onto my butt, two large hands grab hold of me to keep me upright. When I look up, I meet my neighbor's eyes, and my bottom lip trembles.

"What's wrong, Leah?"

Why does he have to be nice right now? It would be easier if he were being a grouch but he looks genuinely concerned.

Do not cry. Don't do it.

My shoulders drop, and big fat tears start rolling down my cheeks. "My dishwasher is broken. I tried to fix it and the videos told me how to fix it, but they all lied in the videos because it's not a stupid gasket and now I have a swimming pool in my kitchen, and I still don't know what's wrong and I feel so stupid and dumb."

He stares at me for a long moment, probably trying to figure out what the hell I just rambled about.

"Okay. Leah, baby, take a breath."

I suck in a breath and let it out. "And Silas told me I should have gone to you to have you fix it, but I told him I could do it and I can't do it because I don't know anything about dishwashers and YouTube lies, and I don't want to bother you because I'm a strong independent woman, but I can't fix the dishwasher, and all I wanted to do today was clean and make my house look like a home for the first time since I've moved in, but every day something else seems to go wrong and I can't handle it."

I'm practically wailing at this point, and my words are incoherent because I can't stop sobbing or get myself together.

Jaxon steps inside, scoops me up in his arms, and carries me like a baby over to my couch.

He carries me like a baby. Me! How the hell the man is able to lift me, I have no idea. He'll probably have a bad back now.

When he sits down, he sets me on his lap and cradles me against his chest as tears streak down my face. My dishwasher isn't to blame for this meltdown. Not entirely, anyway. It's everything that's been building. I bit off more than I could chew with this house, and I don't know what to do.

"I got you, Little one. Take some deep breaths for me. Shh. That's it. Just relax and breathe."

The way he speaks in such a low—but deep—voice soothes me more than I'd like to admit. It feels like a soft stuffy in a way, surrounding me and making me feel safe. Tears continue to fall, but I'm no longer sobbing. Instead, I'm breathing like he told me to do and snuggling into his warm chest. He smells good, too. Like a man. Something woodsy. I move my hand to his beard and run my fingers through it, petting him like I would a soft toy. He doesn't say anything or stop me. He just talks gently to me while I cry. Gosh, I'm such a damn baby.

It takes a while before I'm all cried out and feeling sleepy in his warm embrace. Jaxon is looking down at me and I wonder what he must think of me. Does he think I'm weak? Or stupid for buying this house? I'm not sure but the way he's staring at me makes me feel warm inside. There's no judgment in his gaze, which makes me feel a bit better.

Jaxon

"I'm sorry," I murmur.

I try to sit up in his arms, but his firm grip keeps me cradled like a baby. "Don't apologize, baby. We all have our breaking point. Sometimes Little girls just need a good cry to feel better."

I guess I do feel a little better. My dishwasher is still broken but I'm a little bit lighter inside. Although, that's the only thing light about me and I'm probably hurting Jaxon. I try to wiggle free again and end up letting out a gasp when my bottom shifts against something long and hard. Unless he's carrying a big fat flashlight in his pants, he's sporting a monster erection.

Heat fills my cheeks as I freeze. Jaxon groans and helps me sit up. I immediately stand, keeping my eyes diverted from his…flashlight.

"Leah," he says roughly.

I turn to face him. My cheeks must be flaming red right now. Is he aroused by *me*? That's the million dollar question. A man like Jaxon could get any woman he wants. He's tall, strong, kind—you know, under the gruff exterior—he has a house and a career. I can't imagine the man could be attracted to me.

"Look at me. My eyes, not my chest."

I immediately obey his command because for some reason, I want to please this man.

"Here's what's going to happen. I'm going to fix your dishwasher. You're going to put on music and clean your house like you wanted to. After I'm done, I'm going to check on all your other appliances to make sure they're working fine."

"No, Jaxon. This is your weekend. You don't want to spend your Sunday fixing your neighbor's appliances."

His eyes darken and he stands. When he takes three steps toward me, my heart starts racing. He tips my head back by hooking his index finger under my chin and I practically melt at the dominant gesture. Everything about this man screams power. And I am absolutely here for it.

"You, Little girl, don't tell me what I do and don't want to do. If I didn't want to be here helping you, I wouldn't be. I won't pretend I'm not going to check the game scores on my phone throughout the day, but I want to help you. I need to do this so I can sleep at night knowing you're not going to do something dangerous trying to fix stuff. Are we clear?"

My eyes roam over his face. All the hard lines, dark features, panty-melting lips. I have no idea why he wants to help me or why he even cares but I don't want to think too deeply about it right now, so I nod. "Yes."

He stares at me for a few beats, his eyes searing my skin. "Good girl."

Without another word, he goes to the kitchen and gets to work on my dishwasher. I grab the TV remote. Instead of turning on music, I find a channel that has football on and turn up the volume so he can hear. I don't mind seeing men in tight pants. It's no hardship for me and if it makes the day more enjoyable for him, it's a win win. He's doing me a huge favor, after all.

I spend the next several hours scouring the bathrooms, cleaning windowsills, and wiping down walls in the rooms I still need to paint. The entire house smells like disinfectant and Windex. When I'm satisfied with everything at eye level, I look around for something else to clean. Jaxon moved from my dishwasher to my oven, then my dryer. Every once in a while, I hear him yelling at the TV. He's even let out a few swear words that make me giggle because I'm pretty sure his team is losing.

After finding my duster, I grab a step stool from the garage and go into my room to start dusting the light fixtures. I don't know who lived here before but I'm pretty sure spiders were their best friends based on the number of cobwebs in this house. Yuck!

Jaxon

I'm in the bedroom closest to the living room dusting away when all of a sudden, I feel woozy. The room tips sideways. Unable to stop myself, I fall and land on my tailbone with a thud. I cry out in pain.

Even through my pain, I hear Jaxon's heavy footsteps as he runs into the room, his eyes moving wildly. I expect him to scold me. To yell at me. He doesn't do either of those things. Instead, he comes to me and kneels, his hands running all over my body like he's searching for something.

"Are you okay, baby? Where do you hurt? Fuck. I'm going to take you to the hospital."

Okay, that's not what I was expecting. His big hands roaming my body does things to me. Like turning me on big time. This has got to stop before I do something to embarrass myself.

"Jaxon, I'm okay. I just got a little dizzy. I'm fine."

His hands freeze, and his eyes flick to mine, full of disbelief. "How can you be fine? You fell off the fucking stool. I heard you fall, and you cried out. It must have hurt."

With a sigh, I shrug. "My bottom is the only thing that hurts. I guess it's a good thing I have so much cushion back there."

He lets out a low growl. "Leah."

His voice is so full of warning, goosebumps rise over my body. The man can scold without even trying.

"Why did you get dizzy? And why the hell were you on the stool? I was right in the other room, I could have reached whatever you needed."

"I don't know why I got dizzy." Maybe answering the first question will distract him from the second question. He seems to have a thing with me climbing on stuff.

He narrows his eyes and lets out a huff. "Goddammit, Leah. You're giving me gray hair. I told you not to climb on shit. I swear to God, Little girl, you need a fucking keeper and a red ass."

As soon as the words come out of his mouth, he sighs and shakes his head. "Sorry. I shouldn't have said that," he grumbles.

I scramble to my feet, and Jaxon immediately grabs hold of my wrists like he's worried I'm going to fall again. The man is so sweet at times and such a big, grumpy jerk other times.

"I'm fine. I can stand by myself."

He grunts and lets go of me. "What have you eaten today?"

Crap. I already know he's not going to like the answer. "Uh, coffee?"

His eyebrows pull together and the glare he's shooting my way is a little terrifying. Okay, a lot terrifying.

"Coffee? Was that a question? You aren't sure if you've had coffee? And just FYI, coffee doesn't count as a meal, Leah. You need food. It's nearly two in the afternoon and you're living off coffee? Not acceptable. Get your butt in the kitchen. I'm making you something to eat and while I do that, you and I are going to have a discussion about your fetish with climbing on things."

With a sigh, I tiptoe past him. "Great. Can't wait for that conversation."

"Little girl," he growls.

Yeah, I really need to learn to keep my mouth closed.

10

JAXON

The urge to pull this Little girl's panties down, tip her over my knee, and spank her beautiful round bottom until she promises to never climb on a single thing again—not even a fucking curb—is strong. She needs a paddling more than any woman I've ever met. And the fact that she hasn't eaten all day just adds to my urge to punish her. If she were mine, she would be on a strict eating schedule.

She's not mine, though.

I need to keep reminding myself of that. After everything I went through with Wendy, I have no business getting involved with anyone else. I might be a hermit but at least I won't get hurt again.

Leah has her bottom lip stuck out in a pout as I look through her fridge for sandwich materials. I make lunch for both of us, and she watches me with uncertainty. She knows I'm about to lecture her. With each passing second of silence, she squirms a little more.

Finally, I clear my throat. "How long have you been on your own?"

She definitely wasn't expecting that question. She furrows her eyebrows at me. "What do you mean?"

"I mean, how long since you've had a caretaker?"

Her eyes lower to what I'm doing with my hands as I make our sandwiches. While I want to demand she look me in the eyes while we talk, I don't.

"Uh, well, I've been living by myself for the past six months. Before that I lived in the same house as my ex-husband but we'd been separated for nearly a year before that."

"Was he your Daddy?"

She pulls her plump bottom lip between her teeth as she shrugs. "In the beginning, I guess. It only lasted a year or so before he got less and less interested in being my Daddy — and also my husband apparently based on all the women he cheated on me with. He didn't want a broken wife who couldn't give him what he wanted."

I let out a low growl. My knuckles turn white gripping the knife. I hate the bastard and I don't even know him.

"Your ex is an asshole. A real man doesn't cheat on his wife. You deserved better."

Her watery eyes meet mine and she smiles softly. "Thank you."

"Why would you think you're broken?"

She stares down at her hands and swallows. "I have PCOS."

I continue to stare at her because while I'm pretty sure I've heard the term before, I have no clue what it means. "What is that?"

"It's Polycystic Ovary Syndrome. Basically, it's a hormonal disorder that causes issues with my ovaries. There're a lot of side effects that come along with it, one of which is difficulty getting pregnant. After being married for a couple of years, he decided he wanted kids, and I couldn't get pregnant."

Jaxon

Her voice is so fucking sad that I can't stop myself from reaching over to wrap my hand around one of hers.

"Just because you have a condition doesn't mean you're broken, sweet girl. Your ex was a jackass. Did you guys talk about wanting kids in the beginning?"

She shakes her head. "No. I've known I've had PCOS since I was a teen, and I knew getting pregnant would be very difficult. I also never really wanted kids. It sounds selfish but I knew kids would take away from the time I had for being Little and for me, being Little is a form of therapy sometimes."

Her bastard of an ex needs his ass kicked. The thought of taking him to one of my construction sites and burying him there is really appealing right now.

"First of all, you're not broken. Everyone has different things in life they go through. If someone were missing a leg, would you think they were broken?"

She shakes her head. "No. I would think they were strong for going through whatever it was they went through and living their life despite missing a leg."

"Exactly. You're strong, Little one. Whatever shit your ex fed you about your condition is a bunch of bullshit. It's not your fault you didn't get pregnant. He knew what the chances were when you got together and he knew you didn't want kids. While he's allowed to change his mind about that, he went about it the wrong way and you deserved so much better."

Her body is practically sagging into my side, so I let go of her hand and wrap my arm around her shoulders, squeezing gently.

"You said there're a lot of side effects to PCOS. Like what?"

"It's all embarrassing stuff."

I reach over with my free hand and capture her chin so I

can turn her face to look at me. "Good thing I don't give a shit about embarrassing stuff. Tell me."

With a sigh, she lowers her eyes from mine and stares at my beard instead. "I get whiskers on my chin."

"So you're telling me I have to up my beard game?" I ask, trying to lighten the mood.

Thankfully it works because she giggles and shakes her head. "Your beard is already perfect. But no, I get my face lasered so I don't have to deal with it."

I chuckle, glad she likes my beard. "Okay. What else?"

"I get really painful periods that last longer than normal. Sometimes I can barely even move because the pain is so severe. I also get acne. My weight is a side effect. No matter how hard I diet or exercise, I can't lose weight."

"You're perfect the way you are. You're healthy and lush and beautiful. You don't need to lose a single fucking pound."

That makes her eyes flick to mine, wide and searching, and I know I said too much. Fuck. She's so goddamn beautiful, but I need to keep that shit to myself. She's my neighbor, for fuck's sake, and I'm not looking to date her. I wouldn't mind fucking her and indulging her Little side a bit but that's a bad idea. I can't go there with her.

"What else?" I ask.

She shrugs. "Getting pregnant is difficult obviously. Depression. Hormone imbalance. It's a mess. I'm a mess."

Those words make me growl, and I have half a fucking mind to put her over my knee. "You're not a mess and I don't ever want to hear you say that again. You're human. Everyone has their challenges and that doesn't make them a mess or less than perfect as they are. You're a strong woman, Little bear."

It's silent for a long moment before Leah lets out a huff. "Who knew my grumpy next door neighbor would be such a motivational speaker."

Jaxon

"Hey, I'm a likable guy. Full of wisdom and advice."

That makes her burst out laughing and I don't even care that it's at my expense.

"With all that being said, since you don't have a keeper, Little girl, you need to make better choices for yourself until you find one. That means eating throughout the day and for God's sake, stop climbing on shit. Call me and I'll reach whatever you need."

We start to eat in silence, and I watch her out of the corner of my eye to make sure she's not just nibbling like a bird at her food.

"What about you? What happened with your ex-wife?" she asks.

Everything inside me tenses, and I have to force myself to breathe. Talking about my marriage is my least favorite thing to do but this woman told me her hurts, so I owe it to her to tell her mine.

"I met Wendy in high school. We were friends over the years. It's a small town so everyone knows everyone. She and I started dating in our twenties. She was submissive and had Little tendencies so I introduced her to DD/lg. We practiced it full time for years and I thought she was happy. I thought we were both happy. On our seventh wedding anniversary, she was in the shower and her phone was going off repeatedly, so I picked it up. There was a string of text messages from a man she'd been having an affair with. They had hooked up earlier that day."

Suddenly the sandwich has absolutely no appeal, and I feel like I have sand in my mouth. It makes me sick to talk about the woman who broke me.

Leah has stopped eating and stares at me with wide, wet eyes.

"What a fucking bitch," she finally snaps.

I shoot her a look. "Language, Little girl," I mutter softly. "And yes, what a fucking bitch."

"Why would she do something like that?"

"Because according to her, I was stifling her. I gave her too many rules and not enough breathing room. Apparently, I gave her enough room to breathe that she was able to have a year-long affair before I found out, though."

She shakes her head. "Where is she now?"

This makes me chuckle. "She's currently going through divorce number three. I was her first marriage. It seems as though every man she marries stifles her."

Leah's small hands ball into fists and she shakes her head. "I really want to punch her."

My heart warms at the fierceness she's showing in my defense. The feeling is mutual because I want to punch her ex too.

"She's in the past. I went through a really dark time right after things ended and the only thing that helped me get out of it were my friends. They've always been there for me."

She smiles. "That's good. Silas seems really nice."

Even though he's my best friend, for some reason I don't like her thinking of him as a nice guy. Does she want to date him? That leaves a bad taste in my mouth. Silas is a great man, but Leah is mine.

Fuck. No. She's not mine. Nope. Not a chance. I need to change the subject because otherwise I might end up going over to Silas' house to punch him in the jaw for being *nice*.

"I need you to take better care of yourself, Leah. I might only be your neighbor, but I care about your well-being."

"You're very confusing, you know. One second you're all growly like a hungry bear and the next minute you're saying you care about my well-being. Which I find a little interesting considering Mrs. Jackson across the street said you haven't spoken to her once in the five years since you moved in."

"I guess we've never really crossed paths."

Leah raises an eyebrow. "Mr. Loren said you glare at him

whenever he waves hello."

Shit. She's onto me. How has she already met all these people? And why are they telling her bad things about me?

"Let's just say since my divorce, I've kept to myself. There was a lot of gossip around town when shit went down with Wendy, and she made me out to be this horrible guy. I think most people know the truth but there were some who believed the shit she said. It was easier to be quiet and let the gossip die out but I disconnected from most of the town because I never knew who I could trust."

Her eyes are boring into me. "What makes me so different?"

A smile tugs at my lips. "None of the other neighbors have almost given me heart attacks."

A giggle bursts out of her and I chuckle in response because damn, that laugh of hers is infectious.

"You're going to regret telling me to call you every time I need something from up high, you know. I'm short. I can barely even see over the counter."

She's joking but she isn't far off. She's probably not even five-foot-three. Short and soft and mouthwatering.

"I won't get tired of you. I'll sleep better at night knowing you're not climbing on who knows what."

The sound of her phone interrupts us. She picks it up, grins, and starts typing a message. I wonder what she's smiling about. The insecure side of me hates that I want to know who she's talking to. It's not my business. She's not my girl. She'll never be my girl.

When she puts her phone down, she smiles at me. "Sorry. I met a woman at the hardware store today and she invited me to hang out. She's recently divorced."

"Oh, Natalie?" I ask.

She looks at me for a long moment before she nods. "Yeah. She offered to introduce me to some of her friends since I'm new in town."

"Good. I'm glad. She seems like a good girl. Went through a lot with her asshole ex."

"You know her well?"

The change in Leah's voice makes me glance down at her. Is she jealous?

"No. I met her one night at The Tap Room. Her husband was in her face and Silas and I pulled him away from her. She was crying and he was being a drunk asshole. I'm glad she finally left him. I still want to punch him every time I see the fucker around town."

"Oh. That's so sad. I don't really know her story. We just met but she seemed like she wanted to be friends. I'm excited for that. It's been so long since I've had any."

I raise an eyebrow. "What? Friends?"

She lowers her gaze from mine. "Yeah. He didn't really let me have a social life."

With every new piece of information she tells me about this fucking guy, I want to hunt him down even more.

"That's a form of abuse, Leah. Don't ever let a man keep you from having friends. Okay?"

"Yeah. I know that now."

It's silent in the kitchen besides the faint noise of the football game. I grab our dishes and start to clean up while Leah watches me in a way that makes me think she wants to ask me something. Instead of forcing it out of her, I load the now working dishwasher and wait. She'll ask when she's ready.

"Natalie's really pretty, isn't she?" she finally asks.

"I haven't ever really noticed," I answer without a second thought.

Because it's true. I can't remember what color Natalie's hair is or what color her eyes are or anything about her other than her name. If I saw her, I'd recognize her but when I close my eyes, I can't picture her. The only woman I can see when I close my eyes is the one sitting in this kitchen and that's both terrifying and intriguing.

11

LEAH

"Thank you again for everything today."

Jaxon grunts and steps out to my front porch. "I'll be over tomorrow morning with some guys to start patching your roof. We're not expected to get rain this next week."

I nod, shifting from foot to foot. Mostly because I've spent the better part of the day with this man, bared my soul to him, as he did with me, and now I feel like a school girl waiting to be kissed.

He glances down at my bare feet and lets out another grunt. "You need to get inside and get warm. The temperature is going to start dropping. I'm sure we'll have snow before Thanksgiving this year."

"I am inside," I reply with a smirk.

I love messing with him. He's so easy to rile and even though he just grunts in response, I don't mind it. His caveman noises are growing on me.

"Goodnight, Leah. Call me if anything breaks or you need to reach something."

Yeah, I probably won't do that, but I smile anyway and give Willie a scratch behind the ears before they make their way across our driveways. With one last wave, I close the door and let out a deep sigh. Being around that man all day has been hell on my body. I respond to him in a way I've never responded to anyone in my life.

He made it clear that he isn't getting into a relationship ever again, which is just fine by me. After the crap I went through in my marriage, I don't have the desire to jump into anything either. It's just that it's been so long since I've been touched in a way that makes me feel sexy. And Jaxon Sawyer makes me feel sexy. He also makes me feel Little. The best of both worlds.

Since my house is spotless and nothing is currently broken or leaking, I make my way into my bathroom and turn on the water in the tub. I'll just have to take my attraction to Jaxon into my own hands. Literally. With a vibrator, of course. And bubbles. Can't forget the bubbles.

ON FRIDAY when I get off work, I pull my phone from my purse to see what Natalie has to say.

> Natalie: Want to go out for drinks with me and a couple of my friends tomorrow? They'd love to meet you. They're all Littles too.

I smile. Natalie and I have been texting every day since I met her at the hardware store, and I feel like we're becoming fast friends. We've even sent pictures of some of our favorite stuffies back and forth and talked about everything from sex to our shitty marriages to what we like to do in Little Space. We seem to fall around the same age when we regress, and I love that. There are a fair number of age players who prefer to stay around the Middle ages, but I tend to go much younger. Natalie does too.

> Leah: Sure! What should I wear?

> Natalie: I'm going to wear a pleated skirt.

> Leah: Oh, I love pleated skirts! I have several.

> Natalie: Yes! Wear one with me. We can be twinsies!

Her enthusiasm makes me grin like a fool. Even though Natalie is much prettier than me and has a way better body, I love that she wants to dress alike. And hey, at least I won't feel totally out of place if she's wearing the same outfit.

> Leah: Perfect. I have a light pink one I'll wear.

> Natalie: Eeeek! I have a light purple. We're going to be so cute.

We work out the details and for the rest of the day I feel like I have a pep in my step. I knew life would be hard when I left my ex, and for a while it was, but day by day it's getting so much better.

Jaxon and a couple of his men were over at my house for three days straight this week patching my roof. He was able to fix it well enough that I'll be able to hold off on replacing the whole thing until summer. That was a huge relief. The big grump wouldn't let me pay him a dime for the work he did, though. When I tried arguing about it, he crossed his big, thick arms over his chest and let out some sort of caveman noise. So now that I'm home from work, I'm just going to slip a check into his mailbox. That will show him.

I have no idea if I wrote the check for enough, but he wouldn't tell me how much it cost so I took my best guess. As soon as I close his mailbox door, I hustle toward my house, but the sound of a door slamming stops me in my tracks.

"Little girl!" he roars from his porch.

Shoot. I didn't think he was home.

I turn and offer an innocent smile as I wave at him. "Oh. Hey, Jaxon! Happy Friday! Are you excited for the weekend?"

My fake enthusiasm does nothing to make him stop glowering as he stomps toward me. Uh oh. He doesn't look happy. His eye is doing a twitchy thing, and his tree trunk arms are crossed over his chest.

"What do you think you're doing, Little girl?" he demands.

"Uh, well, I was going home? Like most people do after work. You know, they drive home," I use my hands to pretend I'm steering a car, "and then they park and then they go inside and eat dinner and watch TV or something. Have you never heard of it?"

He makes an exasperated noise, clearly unimpressed with my pretend driving, and practically lasers right through me with his stare. "What were you putting in my mailbox?"

Crap. Why did he have to see that? Was he watching out his window for some reason? Maybe he should find a hobby so he doesn't sit and stare outside all the time. That's just sad.

"Oh, well, um, I put a glitter bomb in there. It's a prank. I'll go get it out now," I say as I make my way back to his mailbox.

"Freeze."

That single, deep command makes me stop. He strides past me and yanks his mailbox open so hard I'm kind of surprised the door didn't come right off the hinge. He holds up the check I just put in there moments ago. Crap. His eye is twitching again.

"What is this?" he demands.

I smile. "Oh, it's called a check. It's like money but

instead of actual money, you take it to your bank and give it to them and they give you money in return."

My Little is hovering just below the surface. If he gets to be grumpy, I can be bratty, right?

"I know what a check is, Little girl. You're riding a very fine line right now. I may not be your Daddy, but I have no qualms about scolding you until you're a very sorry Little girl. Now, why did you put a check in my mailbox? It couldn't possibly be for me fixing your roof when we already settled that I didn't want any payment from you. In fact, I insisted on it."

All my girly parts are fully awake now. My pussy is drenching my panties, practically begging him to scold me while my nipples are so hard they could cut glass. Then again, it's also pretty damn cold outside.

"And why the hell don't you have a coat on? It's thirty degrees outside!"

Of course he would notice I don't have a coat on. The man is much too observant.

"Right, well I should go inside then. That way I don't freeze. You might want to go inside too because the vein in your forehead is pulsing, and I think it's because it's cold out."

I start backing away but with each step toward my house, Jaxon takes one too until we're both on my porch and he is looming over me. The check is crumpled up in his fist and his eyes are so dark they almost look black.

Yikes.

I probably need to soothe the beast instead of aggravating him more.

"I'm sorry. I just feel bad that you did all that work and wouldn't let me pay you anything. You brought employees with you, and you had to get materials so I know it came out of your pocket and I'm just your neighbor so I should pay for the work."

Something flashes in his eyes and his jaw clenches. It seems like what I said pissed him off even more, but I genuinely don't know why that would have made it worse.

"I thought we were friends," he finally says in a quiet voice.

I swallow thickly as a lump forms in my throat. Of course a man like Jaxon would just want to be my friend. He can have any woman he wants. There's no way he would want me. And it shouldn't hurt my feelings that he only wants me as a friend. We barely know each other. We've hung out a couple of times and those were basically forced upon him.

It takes me a minute before I can respond without my voice cracking. "Right. Yep. Yes. We're f-friends. Yep."

His gaze softens and his shoulders relax slightly before he gives me a stiff nod. "So stop trying to pay me. Got it?"

"Yeah. Okay. But like, if you ever need someone to watch Willie or clean your house or something, I'd be happy to do it. Friendly favors and all."

Another grunt. "Start wearing a damn coat. It's not supposed to get above forty degrees for the foreseeable future."

Don't say it, Leah. Don't do it. Just shut up.

"You don't have a coat on."

His eyes narrow, making me shrink back a little.

"That's because I saw my naughty neighbor stuffing something into my mailbox when she wasn't supposed to. Plus, I'm a hell of a lot bigger than you."

That's true. He *is* bigger than me. I wonder if he's big everywhere. I bet he is. My eyes travel down to his boots. Yeah, I bet he's huge just like his feet. Sheesh.

"What size are your feet?" I blurt out.

My eyes widen as I slap my hand over my mouth. For the first time since Jaxon came out of his house, he looks fully amused.

Jaxon

"I just mean, because, like, your feet are really big, and I didn't know they made shoes that big."

His lips pull back into a smile, and he takes a step off my porch. "They're as big as they look, Little one. In case you haven't noticed, everything about me is big. *Everything*."

And then he stalks back to his house like he didn't just drop a big ol' fat bomb on me. Holy fuckadoodle. Was he talking about his feet? Or the other thing?

GOING out with Natalie and her friends is an exciting new adventure for me, but I'm nervous as heck. I don't remember the last time I went out. What if her friends don't like me? This is a small town, and I'm the newbie. If I don't fit in, I'll be a loner for the rest of my life. I bought a house here. It's not like I can just up and move if the town decides I'm not Pine Hollow material.

I've picked up my phone at least a dozen times today to text Natalie and back out of our plans but every time, I end up putting it back down. I want friends. Little friends would be even better. The fact that there is a group of women here who are Littles is a sign. Right? I feel like it's a sign. I lived in Portland for years and the only time I met any Age Players was when I went to Twisted to play. Meeting Natalie out in the wild makes me feel like she's meant to be my friend.

Now, I'm standing in front of the full-length mirror in my bedroom, picking apart my entire outfit. My thighs are pale and jiggly. My hips cause my skirt to flare out. The white long-sleeve shirt I'm wearing only comes down to the waistband of my skirt, so if I lift my arms or move in a weird way, a sliver of my tummy shows. I don't like it. I should probably just change into a pair of jeans and a tunic sweater, but I don't want to disappoint Natalie. We're supposed to be twinning.

Deep breaths, Leah. Just go and have fun.

Easier said than done, right? After giving myself one last glance and making sure the back of my skirt is long enough to cover my panties, I fish out my favorite pair of block-heeled Mary-Janes and put them on. I look like a schoolgirl but, honestly, I love it. Dressing up like this is so fun. I can pass as an adult or a Little in this outfit. I thought about wearing pigtails but opted for a high ponytail with a pink bow that matches my skirt. Pigtails would probably be a little too over the top.

As I make my way out to my car, the sight of Jaxon in dark jeans, a flannel, and a pair of boots greets me. The man looks like a sexy lumberjack. A Daddy lumberjack.

He does a double take when he sees me. His eyes wander up and down my body with hunger before his face morphs into a scowl.

"Where the hell is your jacket?" he demands.

A shiver runs over my body at his scolding tone. There is seriously something wrong with me. Why do I love when this man scolds me? I've never considered myself a brat, but maybe for him I am.

"Oh, um, I forgot to grab one."

He sighs and crosses his thick arms over his chest. "Go get a jacket. Jesus. It's fucking freezing out here and you don't have a jacket," he gestures to my legs, "or pants on."

The urge to roll my eyes and stomp my foot at him is strong but, honestly, I'm not totally convinced Jaxon won't throw me over his shoulder and march me right back into my house if I disobey him. When he doesn't budge, I spin around and go back inside to grab a jean jacket. He grumbles under his breath when I come back out. I suspect he doesn't like the coat I chose.

"Where are you going?" he asks.

His jaw flexes as he scans me up and down again. He looks hungry but also a little pissed off.

"I'm going to The Tap Room with Natalie and some of her friends," I reply cheerily. "What about you?"

A low sound of disapproval rumbles up from his chest. "Poker night with the guys."

I'm not sure why, but I feel my entire body relax. He looks so nice, part of me thought maybe he was going out on a date. Then again, Jaxon did tell me relationships weren't for him after his ex fucked him over, so I don't know why I thought that. Relationships aren't for me either, so I don't know why I felt a pang of jealousy.

"Oh. Well, you look nice. I should go," I murmur.

He sighs. "Your legs are going to freeze."

The man seriously has a hang up about the temperature.

I turn back to him and smile sweetly, adding just a tad more sugar into my tone than normal. "Good thing I'll be inside then. Besides, after a few drinks, I won't feel a thing."

With that, I get into my car and slam the door, then give him a finger wave before I pull away from my house. If he can be difficult and stubborn, so can I.

12

JAXON

She looks like a goddamn wet dream and she's going to The Tap Room on a Saturday night. With those thick legs on display for every man to drool over. Leah Day has no clue how gorgeous she is. I know and I really want to ditch poker night and go to the bar so I can punch every guy who approaches her.

Why am I feeling possessive over my neighbor? I'm not a relationship guy. Sure, I want to fuck Leah. My cock has been hard for her since the night I met her in that damn bear onesie. Not only do I want to do filthy and depraved things to her, I want to spank her round ass for being such a damn brat. The woman needs a keeper. She needs rules and discipline. She needs someone to look out for her and make her wear a damn coat.

Irritated with myself, I head over to Dane's house. Everyone is already there, and the smell of pizza and wings fills the space.

"Hey, man." Dane hands me a beer. "What's with the pissed-off look?"

"That's just his face," Asher says.

I glare at him, then scrub a hand over my face. Silas is staring at me with a smug expression.

"Some Little neighbor is getting Jaxon's panties in a bunch," Silas answers.

Why is this man even my friend? I have no clue, but I need to rethink that.

"Oh, I heard about her. Heard she's a real smoke show, too," Asher replies.

I scowl and then level my gaze at Silas. He's about to get the shit beat out of him. Why the fuck is he calling my girl a smoke show in front of other guys?

Silas holds his hands up defensively. "Hey, I didn't fucking say it. Talk to Cole. He's met her at The Rusty Screw at least a dozen times."

My glare moves from Silas to Cole who is smirking. I wonder how proud of himself he's going to be when I pound him into the ground.

Cole shrugs. "I mean, she's damn hot. And she's trying to do all this DIY shit herself. Asking me questions about the difference between a ratchet wrench and a socket wrench. It's fucking cute, man."

At this point, I'm pretty sure my expression is murderous because Silas elbows Cole to shut up. I set my beer on the counter with a loud clank.

"I'm going to The Tap Room. Anyone who isn't a fucking asshole can join me. Otherwise fuck you all."

The entire room erupts into laughter as I stride out of the house but before I can get in my truck, everyone else heads for their vehicles too.

"I'm guessing she's at the bar tonight?" Silas asks.

"Man, I never thought I'd see the day when Jaxon Sawyer was all bent out of shape over a woman again," Gage says.

Both of the men laugh when I give them the finger before I climb into my truck.

Jaxon

The bar is packed when we arrive and, as soon as we walk in, I scan the crowd for Leah. She's short so it takes me a few minutes to lay eyes on her. Natalie, Bree Doyle, and Greer Bennett, Dane's sister, are standing with her. They each have some bright, sugary concoction in their hands, and they're giggling up a storm. How many drinks have they had?

Dane slaps me on the shoulder. "Shit. Greer already looks buzzed."

Linc grimaces. "Your fucking sister has no sense of self-preservation."

I ignore them and watch as a guy approaches the group. My blood runs cold when he smiles at Leah while he looks her up and down like she's his next meal. She's grinning back at him, laughing at whatever he just told her. I'm across the bar in the blink of an eye, walking right up to Leah.

She looks up at me, shock written all over her face. Those wide blue eyes search mine, and I can tell she's nervous. Her body trembles next to mine, and I barely resist the urge to pick her up and throw her over my shoulder. But if I did, her ass would be on display. My possessive side doesn't want anyone else seeing it.

I level my gaze at Todd, the fucker who's staring at Leah like he's in love. I hate this guy. He was a football star in high school and now thinks he's the ladies' man of Pine Hollow.

"Get lost," I say.

His eyebrows shoot up. "What the fuck, Sawyer? I'm just meeting the newest member of the town. Wanted to offer to show her around."

Silas, Dane, Linc, Gage, Asher, Cole, and Austin walk up and settle themselves among all the women. It's a fucking pissing war between us and Todd, but he gets the point and scoffs as he stomps off to his group of idiot friends.

"Jesus, why don't you just pull your dicks out and

compare sizes with the guy?" Greer asks as she smacks Austin in the chest then glares at her brother.

Austin frowns at her. "Language."

Greer rolls her eyes and shakes her head. I move my gaze to Leah who is staring up at me.

"What are you doing here? I thought it was poker night," she says quietly.

"Yeah, it was. We decided to make it a bar night," I reply.

"Are you spying on me, Jaxon?"

Caught red handed. I lower my head so my mouth is close to her ear. "Yes. Now, be a good girl or, so help me, I'll march you into the bathroom and redden your perfect ass. Hell, I should do that anyway for teasing me in this outfit. How many drinks have you had?"

She lets out a gasp. "Two."

I catch a whiff of her hair. She smells like vanilla. So sweet and edible. My own personal dessert. "Do you know how hard you make me, Leah? How badly I want to bend you over the closest piece of furniture and fuck you until you can't stand up straight? Were you coming here tonight in hopes of finding someone to do that? Because the only person taking you home tonight and doing filthy fucking things to you is going to be me."

She's breathing quickly as she stares up at me with her mouth open in the shape of an *O*. She sways slightly and reaches out to fist her hand in my flannel to keep herself steady. I like that I've knocked her off balance.

"Do you like that idea, baby girl? Me flipping your short little skirt up over your bottom and ripping your panties down so I can fuck you hard and deep?"

A small whimper escapes her lips, and her eyes are glazed over as she gives the tiniest of nods. Everyone around us is deep in conversation and not paying attention to what we're doing, so I reach for her free hand and pull it toward my aching erection.

Jaxon

When her palm makes contact with the front of my jeans, her eyes widen and she molds her hand around my cock. I groan at the simple touch.

"This is what you do to me, Little girl. You drive me fucking crazy. I've wanted to fuck you since I saw you in that tight little bear onesie."

Her hand tightens around my dick and, at the same time, she's gripping my shirt for dear life.

"Do you want me to take you home tonight and make you come apart, Leah? Do you want to be Daddy's good Little girl for the night?"

I know I'm going to regret this tomorrow. She's my neighbor. I don't do relationships. I'll make sure she knows this will only be a physical thing but it's still risky. Right now, though, I can't seem to find a single fuck to give. Her hands on me are making it impossible to think straight and the electricity I've been feeling with her since we met is like a lightning bolt hitting us right now.

She finally nods.

"I need to hear the words, baby."

She hasn't said a single thing since I've been whispering my dirty fantasies in her ear. While I might have bulldozed her with what I want, I won't act on it unless it's what she wants too.

"Yes. I want that," she whispers just loud enough for me to hear.

"I can only be your Daddy for one night, baby. I don't do relationships. I don't have it in me."

"I know. I don't either. Just tonight. It's been so long," she replies breathily.

Knowing it's been a long time for her makes my dick throb against her hand. What the hell is wrong with me? The last time I felt so damn possessive over a woman was my ex-wife and it's terrifying. I know after I fuck Leah, I won't feel this way. She'll be out of my system. After tonight these feelings will disappear. They always do.

I smile and slide my hand to her bottom, thankful for the shitty lighting and the high-top table blocking the view of our hands. Her ass feels so perfect in my palm, and I can't wait to turn it red later. I give it several firm pats as I lean down to her ear again.

"You be a good girl for the rest of the night, and I'll reward you when we get to your place. No more drinks. I want you clear headed when I worship your beautiful body later. If I see you flirt with any other men tonight, I'm going to take you out to the parking lot, bend you over the seat of my truck and spank your bottom until you're a very sorry Little girl. Understand?"

Another gasp escapes her, and she squeezes my cock again. If she doesn't stop with that, I'm going to come before we even leave this bar.

"Yes," she moans.

I want her to have a good time with her friends but damn, I also really want to drag her out of here right this second and fuck her every which way.

"Good girl. I'm going to make you feel so good. I can't wait to see what panties you have on under that skirt. I bet they're fucking adorable. Probably as cute as those training panties you had on the other night."

A shiver runs through her so forcefully that I feel it as she sways against me. She shifts from foot to foot, and I realize she's squeezing her thighs together. I'm glad she's turned on too.

"Leah, let's get another round!" Greer calls out.

I pat her bottom and raise an eyebrow at her before she turns her attention to her friend and removes her hands from my body. I miss her touch immediately.

"Oh, just water for me. I'm already too buzzed," she replies, waving her hand dismissively.

"That's Daddy's good girl," I whisper in her ear.

Austin shakes his head. "I think all of you need a round of waters."

I'm glad he has my back on this. "Agreed. You ladies stay here and chat. We'll bring you some waters and food to munch on."

When I remove my hand from Leah's bottom, she lets out a small sound of protest that makes all the blood surge to my cock again. Baby girl likes it when I touch her. Good to know.

13

LEAH

Even though I've only had two drinks, I think I'm drunk. To be totally honest, I'm not sure if it's the alcohol that's making me feel this way. I think it's the six-foot-four beast of a man looking at me from the bar. The one who just had his hand on my bottom and was whispering filthy things into my ear.

The number of times I've fantasized about Jaxon Daddying me is more than all my fingers and toes. My vibrator has been getting a nightly workout. I'm not even sure why I'm attracted to him. He's hot. There's no doubt about it. All the women in the bar are eyeing him like he's the piece of candy they've been searching for all their lives. I kind of want to scratch those women's eyes out. Despite that, he's cranky. Rude. Abrupt. Bossy. His vocabulary is mostly just grunts and growls.

Those are reasons enough why I shouldn't want him. Tell that to my vagina, though. And my bottom. They don't listen to those signs. My kitty is practically mewling for his attention and my lower cheeks are clenching at the thought of him spanking me. I shouldn't want to feel the painful sting, but I do. I want to feel the burn of his palm on my skin while I wiggle and squirm. I want him to make me beg for him to stop even though deep down I won't want him to. I want him to dominate and manhandle me until I'm coming apart for him like he said.

I squirm and shift, squeezing my thighs together for any kind of friction I can get on my swollen clit. I've never been this horny before. The man hasn't even touched me under my clothes yet and I'm on the verge of orgasm.

Thankfully, he made it clear it would only be for tonight. I don't want Jaxon Sawyer for anything more than that. I don't want any man for anything more. I was tied down to my ex and had my life practically taken away before my eyes. It's my turn to start living and having friends. It's my turn to have fun. Even though my nights are lonely, and I crave having a Daddy to help me get ready for bed or do all the things a good Daddy would do for me, it's best if I stay single. I don't want to lose myself again. I let myself be controlled in a way that wasn't healthy.

"Drink, baby girl."

His deep voice draws my attention from my past and I tilt my head back to look up at him. He's staring down at me with so much intensity and dominance that I take the glass from his hands and drink several gulps.

"That's a good girl. Keep behaving and I'll give you many rewards tonight."

Uh, hell yeah. I'll do whatever he tells me if he'll give me said rewards. He grins like he knows what I'm thinking then winks at me. My panties are soaked, and I want to leave with him right this second, but I also don't want to ditch my new friends. Bree, Greer, and Natalie have treated me like I've always been part of their friend group and it's such a cool feeling. I already adore them, and they've even brought up doing play dates.

"The guys and I are going to go over to that table and hang out so you can continue your girls' night. I ordered you all some mozzarella sticks, chips and salsa, and sliders. I'm betting you didn't eat dinner tonight?"

Shoot. Why does he know me so well? It's unnerving. He won't like what I have to say. He takes my silence as an answer and narrows his eyes at me.

"That's what I thought. Eat the food. I mean it. It's not good to drink alcohol on an empty stomach."

I'm swooning over his simple command. He's taking care of me. Just like he had the night I burned my dinner. And the day I climbed up on my roof. And when he fixed my dishwasher.

He's just my neighbor. My hot, dominant neighbor who happens to be a Daddy and who I'm going to fuck tonight. It's casual. Catching feelings is not an option.

"'Kay."

"Good girl. I'll be right over there if you need me. And if any man approaches you and asks you to dance, you send him to my table. The only man putting his hands on your body tonight will be me."

A shiver works its way down my spine. This might only be a one-night stand but I love his possessiveness over me. It's confusing as fuck. I want him, but I don't want to want him in any way other than for my own sexual needs.

After he gives me a pat on my bottom, Jaxon makes his way to the table. I watch him go and, when I turn back to my friends, they're all grinning at me.

"What?" I ask.

Greer laughs. "Just enjoying the show."

Bree snorts. "The show of Leah eye-fucking Jaxon Sawyer."

My mouth drops open. "I was not eye-fucking him."

Natalie practically cackles. "Yeah. And when your hand was groping his crotch? Were you checking his pulse or something?"

Heat rises to my cheeks, and I'm worried I might burst into a ball of flames.

Shoot. I didn't think anyone had seen that.

My friends burst out into giggles so loud I'm pretty sure every single person in the bar looks at us. That makes my cheeks heat even more.

"We're totally teasing you," Natalie says through her giggles. "Jaxon is a good guy. A little uptight sometimes but good. He's a Daddy, you know?"

Uh, yes, I know. How does *she* know? She must realize I'm horrified because she reaches over and places her hand over mine.

"Oh, girl, no. Jaxon is just a friend. He helped me once and I saw him and his friends at Twisted a couple of times. That's the only reason I know he's a Daddy. Well, that, and Dane is Greer's brother. All of the guys over there are Daddies from what we know."

Everything in me relaxes as I look over at the men across the bar. Jaxon's attention is on me despite the conversation happening at their table.

"Does he mess around with a lot of Littles?" I ask.

Why did I ask that? It's not my business and it doesn't matter who or how many women he messes around with, but I want to know.

Greer shakes her head. "Jaxon doesn't mess around with anyone from Pine Hollow. I think the guys make trips out to Twisted every so often. I told my brother he has to tell me when they're going so I don't go on the same night because, ew. If I saw my brother at a sex club, I think I'd have to pour bleach into my eyeballs."

We all giggle.

"So, tell us, are you going to ride Jaxon's dick tonight?" Greer asks.

Greer is definitely the most outgoing of the group. She curses like a sailor too. I love her already. She's the type of

Jaxon

friend who doesn't have a filter, wants to know all the dirty details of peoples lives and would be the first to show up with a shovel if you needed to bury a body.

I bite my bottom lip, wondering if I can trust them with my secrets.

Bree smiles sweetly. "Anything said in this group stays between us. Even though this is a small town and gossip gets around, we try to keep our personal lives private from the gossip mill."

Something tells me these women are going to become my very best friends and I can trust them.

"He's coming to my place tonight. Just for tonight," I admit.

The three of them stare at me, wide-eyed with grins.

"Uh-huh. Just for tonight," Greer finally says.

"Yes. Neither of us want anything more. I just got out of a shitty marriage, and it sounds like his ex really messed with his head. But since we met, there's been this electricity between us. So we're going to have sex and put it to rest. Is neighbors with benefits a thing?"

"You can say it's just for tonight all you want, but the way he's looking at you suggests it's much more," Bree says.

I sneak a glance at him to find him staring at me.

"Nah. It's just physical attraction. And it's been so long since I've had anyone Daddy me. It's just for tonight."

They don't believe a word I'm saying, but I know better. It's only sex. Even though I'm pretty sure his dick is going to ruin me for other men. The man is enormous. It's going to hurt and I'm going to love every painful second of it.

The appetizers he ordered arrive, and I dig into the greasy bar food, enjoying every single bite. My diet can start tomorrow.

"Hey, do you guys wanna get together tomorrow afternoon for movies and snacks? We can play dolls and talk about Leah and Jaxon's sexcapades?" Natalie asks.

Bree and Greer bob their heads enthusiastically while I chew on a mozzarella stick.

"Yes! We should make it a weekly thing. Sunday Funday!" Greer says.

A smile spreads. I like that idea. A weekly girls' day for all of us.

"Definitely. I'll come whenever I can. Between working at the hardware store and the coffee shop, I never really know what my schedule is," Natalie replies with a shrug.

We all agree to make Sunday Funday a thing and to schedule it for a time that Natalie isn't working. Even though I'm playing it cool on the outside, I'm totally doing a happy dance inside. I have friends. They want to hang out with me, and I don't have an asshole ex anymore to take that away.

Around midnight, Jaxon approaches our table. "Time to go, Little bear. It's way past your bedtime."

My friends are grinning like idiots.

"Go have fun! We'll drink more margaritas on your behalf!" Greer says.

The rest of Jaxon's friends have appeared at the table.

Austin shakes his head. "No, you won't. We're driving you home. Don't want you on the road this late."

Greer glares at Austin, and I'm starting to wonder if there's something between them. I need to ask her about it tomorrow during our girls' day.

"We live in Pine Hollow. There isn't even a stop light. I'm pretty sure we'll be fine to drive ourselves," Greer snaps at him.

Both Austin and Dane raise an eyebrow.

"Greer, we're driving you home. You know how we are. We're not going to let you all drive alone in the dark," Dane says.

She rolls her eyes. "Yes, I know how you all are. Overbearing and impossible."

Natalie and Bree both giggle but don't argue as we make

our way out to the parking lot. Jaxon pulls me away from my friends and plants me in the passenger seat of his truck. Seems this hot lumberjack is impatient to get me home.

It's completely silent as he drives. We didn't even talk about the fact that we left my car at the bar. The town is small enough that I could walk to The Tap Room tomorrow to pick it up.

The quiet in the cab of the truck is making me second guess all of this. Are we making a huge mistake? This guy is my neighbor and I'm going to have to see him all the time. Though, you can keep it short and sweet when you do see a neighbor. It's not like we have to hang out. So it's fine. Everything will be fine. Yep. We're totally not heading straight into a dumpster fire.

He pulls into his driveway and parks. "Stay there. I'll come around."

Without waiting for me to agree or argue, he gets out of the truck and walks around to the passenger side to open the door. I love the way he takes control and cares for me in his own grumpy way. It makes my clit tingle.

When he reaches over and unbuckles my seatbelt, I practically start panting. His arm brushes across my nipples. Sheesh. If I'm this responsive now, I can't even imagine how it will be once we're naked.

Shoot! We have to get naked. More importantly, *I* have to get naked. That little thought immediately kills my mood. If he sees me naked, he'll never want to fuck me again. Which maybe isn't a bad thing since we agreed on only one night. But even though it's just a one-time thing, I don't want him to be disgusted by me. I'm wearing a skirt so maybe I can get away with keeping my clothes on and he'll just pull my panties down to fuck me. Yeah. Right. I already know I won't be that lucky.

He walks me to my front door and, as soon as I unlock the door and open it, he grabs my wrist.

"I'm going to go get Willie. In the meantime, I want you to go inside and get a glass of water and drink it. I'll be right back."

He brushes his lips against my forehead and heads toward his house. I scurry inside. Maybe I can light some candles. That way it's dim in the house, so he won't be able to see all my rolls and jiggly thighs.

Yeah, that'll work. After I flip on two lamps to their lowest setting, I decide against lighting a candle. Somehow, I'm pretty sure he'll scold me for playing with fire if I do. The nightlight in my bedroom should be enough in there.

I grab a glass of water and start to drink it as Jaxon appears in my living room with a very excited Willie. The dog's tail is swishing uncontrollably as he runs over to me. His entire body is shaking with enthusiasm. This furball is seriously the total opposite of Jaxon.

"Why's it so dark in here?" he asks.

My cheeks heat because I don't want to tell him the truth. I'm pretty sure he'll know if I'm not being honest, though. I hate that the man can read me so well.

I keep a safe distance away from him, hoping he won't see my red cheeks or diverted eyes as I whisper, "I just wanted to have some mood lighting for us. I thought you'd like it."

He lets out a low growl. "What the hell makes you think that I want all the lights off if I'm going to only have you tonight? I want every single inch of you exposed to me. I want to lick, kiss, and see everything."

A shiver courses through me from head to toe. This man says the filthiest things, and it turns me on like a water faucet. At the same time, I know he probably doesn't really mean it.

He takes a step closer to me. And then another step, and pretty soon, he's right before me looking down into my eyes with a look of disapproval. "You're not telling me the truth, Leah. Why are the lights off. And be honest."

I nibble on my bottom lip and look up at his face, the hard lines, his eyebrows furrowed together, and his stunning eyes. "I just, I think it would be better if the lights were off," I tell him. "That way you won't have to see me naked."

Within a flash, he picks me up by the hips and lifts me onto the kitchen island. He puts his hands on either side of my thighs, boxing me in. His face is only inches from mine. And I can tell that he isn't happy with me at all.

"What in the fuck makes you think I wouldn't want to see you naked? I've been looking at you since the day we met. I can't wait to see you without all your clothes. You're gorgeous, Leah. Every inch of you. And obviously, no one's ever made you feel that way. But I'm going to tonight."

I look down at my hands and pick at my cuticles because I'm not really sure what to say. I'm pretty sure that he's going to look like a chiseled god. And yet, once he undresses me, he's going to see every imperfection I have. It scares me.

His fingers brush under my chin as he tips my head back so I have to look him in the eye. "Baby girl. I want to see you. You're gorgeous and I don't know who put these horrible thoughts in your head, but you're absolutely perfect just the way you are. And I'm going to prove that to you. You need to trust me, though."

I feel like I already do, but at the same time, every nerve and cell in my body is telling me to run, scream, and hide. Not because I'm scared of him, but because I'm scared of *this*. Kevin messed me up so bad in the head. He made me feel so small—and not in the way I wanted.

But Jaxon looks at me like I'm beautiful and he makes me believe it too. I tell him the truth. "I trust you. I'm just scared."

His lips brush my cheek. "I need you to know that you are

the type of woman that I absolutely love. I don't want some skinny woman that I'm gonna break in half when I fuck her hard and fast. I want a woman who has beautiful thick thighs like you do that I can kiss, lick, bite, and grab a hold of. I want to feel your tummy pressed up against me, soft and feminine, and I want your big, beautiful tits right in my face so I can be suffocated by them. Your ass is, fuck, your ass is my nightly fantasy. And I can't wait to lick and bite and suck on each of your cheeks. I can't wait to spank them too. You definitely need to be spanked."

His words practically have me panting. He talks so dirty. And his voice... It's like a drug I'm addicted to, but I know I shouldn't be. This is a one-time thing. Jaxon wants nothing more. I want nothing more. Yep, I'm going to keep telling myself that.

I hesitate for a moment before I reply, "Okay, I trust you."

He smiles in the way that only he can. It's stern but soft. "Good girl. I'm so proud of you. I'll never hurt you, Leah. I will never make you feel like anything but the most beautiful woman in the world. It doesn't matter that tonight's a one-time thing. You always have my respect, and I will always think you're gorgeous. You're absolutely perfect."

If my mouth hadn't already been stone dry, it would be now. Damn, this man is killing me. My panties are drenched, and my breasts are heavy and aching. God, I can't wait to feel him inside me, stretching me to the max.

I offer a smile. He returns it with one of his own then leans forward, brushing his lips against mine. I'm surprised at how soft they are. He's hard, but soft in all the right places, and his lips are definitely no exception. What starts off as a gentle kiss becomes possessive and desperate. We cling to each other. Practically eating each other's mouths as we explore. His hands are all over me. My nails dig into his shoulders as he kisses me like I'm his last meal.

The man can certainly freaking use his tongue. I wonder

Jaxon

what it'll feel like down below. I want to find out. When he pulls away, we're both panting. My hands are still on his shoulders. Even though I'm sitting, I feel like I need him for stability. He's gripping my hips and it's bruising, but I love it. I love the pain mixed with the pleasure.

"What's your safe word, baby girl?"

I nibble on my lip and look at him, unsure what to say. When I don't answer, he cocks his head to the side and looks at me with questioning eyes. "Have you never had a safe word?"

I shake my head. "Kevin told me I didn't need to have one. He said that safe words were for pussies."

Jaxon growls, only this time, it's not one of his quiet ones. He sounds like a bear ready to kill. He clenches his jaw and, when he speaks, it's low and menacing. "That man is going to wish he had a safeword when I get my hands on him. You always need a safeword. It doesn't matter who you're with, how much you trust them, or how long you've been together. Always have a way to stop things. It's not safe if you don't. You never know what could go wrong, and sometimes your Dom may not figure out that there's something wrong until it's too late. Tonight, your word is red. If you feel anxious, scared, hurt, anything that makes you want this to stop, you say red, and it stops immediately. Do you understand me?"

Whoa. Protective Jaxon is pretty damn sexy. "Yes, I understand."

He gives a sharp nod and lifts me off the counter like I weigh nothing. I squeal and wiggle, but he doesn't put me down as he moves toward the back of the house. The entire way, he mumbles about how dark it is and that he hates that he can't see me. It makes me smile. Even though I'm nervous to be naked in front of him, I like that he's so determined about it. There's no question as to what he wants.

The second we walk into my bedroom, he flips on the

overhead light. I let out a squeak. "Wait, can we have a lamp on? Like, something that's not so bright?"

He chuckles and deposits me on the bed. "Give me just a second, baby, and I'll switch it."

Overhead lighting is seriously the worst. The only place it should be legal is in an operating room.

Willie seems content as he finds a place on the bedroom floor, makes several circles, then lies down with a bored sigh.

Jaxon starts unbuttoning his flannel shirt, exposing his broad chest to me all the way down to the waistband of his pants. God, the man is built. He doesn't have a six pack, but he's solid as a brick wall. There's a smattering of hair across his chest and down his tummy, disappearing under his jeans. He eyes me with a smirk.

"You like what you see, baby?"

My cheeks heat. Because yes. I do. He's gorgeous. I can see why every woman in the bar was staring at him tonight, and I wonder if he's ever gone home with any of them. I don't want to think about that, though. I don't want to think about any woman who's ever been with him. Tonight, I'm going pretend I'm the only one in Jaxon Sawyer's life.

14

JAXON

She's staring up at me from the bed like I'm the scariest—yet most interesting—creature she's ever seen. Her sparkling eyes are full of wonder and lust. I can't wait to show her how beautiful I think she is. I don't know how she doesn't get it, but I'm going to prove it to her.

When I step between her legs, her breath hitches, and she leans back slightly. I reach for the hem of her shirt, but her arms tense at her sides so I can't lift it. "Trust me. I want to see you."

With a sigh, she relaxes her arms, and I quickly strip off her top. The white lace bra is barely holding up her breasts. Her skin is so milky, yet her chest and face are flushed. Her nipples press against the material, and I can't stop myself. I kneel in front of her and suck one of the stiff peaks through the fabric.

She lets out a moan as her hand slides up the back of my neck, threading through my hair. "Oh God, Jaxon."

I love the sound of her moan, but tonight, I'm her Daddy.

I pull away from her breasts and meet her gaze. "Baby girl, tonight I want to be Daddy. Do you have any objections to that?"

Her wide blue eyes stay on mine as she shakes her head.

"Good girl. For tonight, you call me Daddy and you obey all of my commands, or you'll be punished. You have your safeword if you need things to stop and you'll never be in trouble for using it. I'm not going to go over all of your limits tonight, but is there a specific limit you want to tell me about?"

She thinks for a moment, chewing on her bottom lip. "I don't want to be tied up."

My eyebrows furrow because the way she says it makes me think something happened that made that a hard limit. "That's fine, baby. I won't tie you up. I might restrain your wrists with my hands. Is that okay?"

She thinks about it for a brief moment. "I think that's fine. Can I say red if I don't like it?"

I reach out and cup her chin firmly, running my thumb over the point. "You can say red any time for any reason. Even if we're just talking and you need it to stop, you can say it."

"Thank you," she whispers.

Her bottom lip trembles slightly. I'm pretty sure her ex did something else shitty to her that he needs to pay for.

"You're very welcome, baby. Just remember, you hold all the power. I might be the one bossing you around, but you're the one who says to stop or go."

I move my thumbs over her nipples. She whimpers and arches into my hand, so I palm both of her breasts. They're beautiful. Heavy and full. They're going to be even more beautiful once I've taken her bra off, but I'm trying to go slow so I can ease her into this. I'm afraid if I move too fast, she's going to chicken out on getting naked for me.

Her tongue darts out, her nose level with my bulging cock. I want her plump lips wrapped around my shaft but that's going to have to wait until later. If her mouth so much as touches me down there, I'll come, and I don't want it to be over that quickly. The first time we have sex, it's going to be with me buried deep in her pussy.

With one swift movement, I reach back and unhook her bra. The material snaps forward, making her gasp, but when I grab the straps and pull it away from her body, she doesn't protest. Her nipples are a deep pink and they're big—the size of silver dollars. It makes my mouth water.

"So beautiful. I want my cock between your big tits as I fuck your chest and give you a pretty pearl necklace."

Her chest rises and falls rapidly. She likes that idea. Another thing to do before the end of the night. At my age, I'm not sure if I can go more than one round but if it's possible, it will be with Leah. She gets my blood racing like no other woman ever has.

"You like that idea, baby? You want Daddy to fuck your pretty tits?" I tug on one of her nipples then give it a sharp pinch. She cries out and throws her head back. I give the other breast the same treatment and soon she's quietly begging for more.

"Please, please, please," she whimpers.

A low chuckle rumbles in my chest. Seeing Leah come apart, even this much, is an unforgettable sight. I have a feeling when she's writhing under me, she'll glow.

I take hold of both of her wrists and pull her to stand with her calves pressed against the bed. Her hands snake up around my neck as I lower my face to hers for a possessive kiss. The feel of her hard nipples against my chest makes my cock ache even more, but I'm only getting started with her.

When our mouths part, we stare at each other for a long moment before I wrap my fist in her ponytail and spin her around to face the bed. It only takes one tug to pull her skirt down her hips to let it drop to the floor. Her white lace briefs match her bra. So sexy yet innocent, just like her.

She looks over her shoulder at me as I press my hand between her shoulder blades.

"Bend over and put your palms on the mattress."

When she obeys, I step back and observe her lush body. The only thing she has on is her panties and those sexy little heels she wore to the bar. Her tits hang toward the mattress and her round ass is full, begging for my attention. I step closer and palm the round globes.

"So pretty. So full and soft, just the way Daddy likes."

The only sounds that come from her are tiny mewls as she wiggles her bottom against my hand. I give her a sharp smack just under the hem of her panties and grin when I see my handprint bloom into a shade of pink on her flesh.

"I should give you a sound bare bottom spanking and not let you come tonight for all the ways you've tortured me. Climbing on the fucking roof and the counter and the goddamn step stool. You need to learn your lesson."

She lets out a sound of protest and shakes her head. "No, please. Please, I'll be good. I promise."

I chuckle and shake my head. "Little girl, don't make promises you can't keep. We both know you're trouble waiting to happen."

Another sharp smack to her bottom makes her cry out.

"I will tell you this, Leah, and I want you to listen carefully. If I catch you climbing up on any other things, I will give you a very serious and harsh spanking. Are we clear?"

Her bottom clenches, but she squeezes her thighs together. She both loves and hates the idea. A common inner battle many Little girls have over being punished.

When she doesn't answer me right away, I spank her bottom several times, hard and fast, alternating cheeks.

"I asked you a question, Little girl. Are we clear?"

"Yes," she whimpers.

Smack! Smack!

"Yes, Daddy, is the appropriate answer."

Smack! Smack!

"Yes, Daddy!"

I smooth my hand over her bottom. "Good girl."

She's panting and shifting from foot to foot and it's the most adorable thing ever. The scent of her arousal fills the room. I've gone as slow as I possibly can at this point. With the hook of my thumb in the back of her panties, I yank them down her thighs then drop to my knees behind her.

Using my thumbs, I spread her glistening pussy lips, pleased with how swollen they are. My girl is wet and needy.

I circle her clit with my fingers, giving the swollen nub several sharp pinches that make her shudder.

"You smell like sugar. I bet you taste even better," I say before I bury my face in her wetness.

She cries out as I run my tongue along her entire pussy. When she wiggles slightly, I smack her ass and grab hold of her hips so she can't move.

"Oh. My. God."

A chuckle rumbles from my chest. My girl likes this attention. I continue to use my mouth on her for several minutes: licking, sucking, and biting. When her body starts to tense and her breathing quickens, I slide two fingers into her pussy and curl them.

"Holy fuck! Daddy! Oh, shit, I'm going to—"

Her climax takes over, and her entire body shudders so violently that her arms give out. Her chest falls to the mattress. I don't stop, though. Instead, I add a third finger and start to pound into her with them as I give her ass several smacks.

"Good girl coming for Daddy. That's it, baby. Fuck my hand. That's it, take what you need, Little one."

She cries out over and over as the walls of her pussy pulse around my digits. I regret making her come the first time in this position because I'm dying to see her beautiful face right now.

As soon as her orgasm subsides, I rise and flip her onto her back so she's staring up at me. Her face is flushed, her eyes are glassy, and her nipples are hard peaks begging for my attention.

Her eyes roam my body, and she pulls her bottom lip between her teeth when her gaze lands on my crotch. My cock is so hard it could cut glass at this point and the restriction of my jeans is painful. When I start to unbuckle my belt, her eyes widen.

"Worried about me taking off my belt, baby? Do I need to use it on your naughty bottom?"

Her head shakes so hard I think she's going to get whiplash and it makes me chuckle. "Easy, baby. No belt tonight. Though, I catch you climbing on any more things and you'll definitely get more than my hand on your bottom."

Several emotions cross her face at once as her eyelashes flutter. She both likes and hates the idea. I hope she hates it enough not to do dangerous shit anymore. Even though tonight is all we'll ever have, I meant what I said about spanking her if she disobeys me.

I unzip my jeans. As soon as my cock is free, jutting toward my stomach, she gasps and squeezes her thighs together.

"That's not going to fit," she whimpers.

I reach for her knees and push them open to expose her gleaming pussy. "It's going to fit, baby. It's going to be tight, but it will fit. Daddy will be very careful."

Vulnerability flashes in her eyes as she looks at me. "Okay."

After I grab a condom from my back pocket, I kick off my boots and step out of my pooled jeans so I'm standing in front of her completely naked. She still wears those fuck-me heels and her thick legs look beautiful with them on.

"Do you want me to, uh?" She motions toward my cock as she starts to sit up.

"Not this time. Maybe later. For right now, I need to be inside you. Are you ready for Daddy?"

15

LEAH

Was that a trick question? I'm more than ready. My body is vibrating with need despite just having an orgasm. And what an experience that had been. Definitely one for the record books.

As he rolls the condom down his hard, thick length, I lick my lips. I've never wanted to suck a man's cock so badly in my life, but I've also never wanted a man to fuck me so badly either.

"Daddy asked you a question. Do I need to put you over my knee and warm your luscious bottom again to get you to pay attention?"

Huh? What? Oh, he wanted an actual answer. Because obviously the waterfall between my legs isn't enough of a sign for him.

"No. I mean, yes. Yes, I'm ready. Please."

He crawls over me and I can't help but watch his heavy cock swinging between his thighs as he moves. I always knew the man had big dick energy. It's the only reason he's able to be such a growly jerk and get away with it.

When he's hovering over me, practically pinning me to the bed with his face just above mine, I meet his gaze. He's a beautiful specimen. What he sees in me, I'm not really sure but I'm not going to question it. I'm going to enjoy it. Inch by glorious inch.

The head of his cock nudges my opening, and my anxiety spikes. I really don't think he'll fit. I've never seen a cock so big that wasn't in a porno. My gaze moves between us to take it in.

"Eyes on mine," he says firmly but quietly.

I obey and quickly relax. Jaxon might hurt my heart, but I trust he'll never harm me.

"That's my girl. Good girl." He captures my lips in a deep kiss that has me moaning into his mouth. At the same time, he nudges forward. I widen my legs for him as much as I can.

It burns at first as his thickness stretches me, but he makes shallow thrusts until his cock is coated in my cream. He starts toying with my nipples. The pain mixes with pleasure, and pretty soon I'm grinding my hips against his, trying to get him to move deeper.

He lifts his head and stares down at me. In one swift thrust, his balls hit my ass.

"Oh!"

"No cursing," he mumbles as he pulls out and thrusts again.

I roll my eyes at him because the man is such a Daddy and I love it. He winks and starts fucking me long and hard.

"Shit, Leah. You're so tight, baby."

My arms are wrapped around his neck, my fingernails scratching the skin on his back. "No cursing," I cry out.

He reaches under us and gives my bottom a light smack that makes me grin as he fucks me.

"The only one giving out the rules around here is me." With each word, he thrusts hard.

"Daddy! Oh! I'm going to come!"

And I do. My body tenses, the room spins, and my pussy

pulses as I scream and cry out for him. His movements become erratic and his thrusts harder as he clenches his jaw.

"Fuck, baby. I'm going to come too." He lets out a low growl. My climax continues to ripple through me while we come together, our cries filling the room.

When he stops moving, I collapse against the mattress in a pile of putty. That was the most intense, life-altering orgasm I've ever experienced and based on the string of whispered curses he's letting out, it might be the same for him too.

I reach up and stroke his hair for a few moments while we lie together. The only sound in the room is our harsh breathing. When that returns to normal, he pulls out of me, and I feel a sense of loss as he gets to his feet. It's stupid. I knew the score. This was a one-time fuck and nothing more. I shouldn't expect any snuggling. I need to suck it up, get out of this bed, and politely walk him to the door like a good host.

He disappears into the bathroom. I jump up to find something to throw on. I grab an oversized T-shirt and just get it over my head when Jaxon walks back into the room.

"What do you think you're doing, Little bear?"

I gape at him, completely confused. "I was putting on clothes so I could walk you out."

Something flashes in his eyes but is gone in an instant and replaced with a firm glare. "Daddy didn't give you permission to get out of bed or to get dressed. Get your cute bottom back over there. I'm going to get you cleaned up and ready for bed. Then we're going to cuddle and watch a movie while I feed you a snack. After that, I'm probably going to fuck you again before we go to sleep."

What. The. Hell? Am I in dreamland? He's planning to clean me up and take care of me? That wasn't part of the deal. It seems like a dream come true and I'm not going to complain, but I'm a bit confused. He takes a single, menacing step forward, and I lunge for the bed. My bottom is still heated from his earlier spanking. I'm not sure I want another, more serious one right now. I have no doubt if I disobey him, he would do just that.

Jaxon gives me a smug smile as he makes his way over to the bed. He towers over me, a washcloth in hand. "Lie back and spread your legs, Little bear. Show me what's mine."

I pull my lip between my teeth and do as he says, happy I was able to get the shirt on before he came back out. At least I'm afforded some sort of modesty.

Kevin never cleaned me up after sex, so this is new and unusual, but such a turn on. It makes me feel cared for in a way that I'm not used to. I'm unsure how to feel about it, emotionally. My kitty thinks it's hot. My heart? I'm not so sure.

Jaxon cleans me up, wiping me from front to back. I wiggle when his finger hits my back hole and my eyes flick to his. He just winks and removes the cloth from my skin.

"Do you want to sleep in training panties or a diaper, baby girl?"

My heart pounds in my chest and my cheeks burn. "I can just sleep in panties."

He raises one eyebrow. "I didn't ask if you wanted to sleep in panties. I asked if you wanted to sleep in a diaper or training panties. Pick one."

I know I won't get away without answering him but sheesh, it's hard to respond. "Training panties, please."

He motions toward the dresser. "Which drawer?"

After several seconds of digging in the one I pointed him to, he pulls out a pair of training panties. "Normally I wouldn't give you a choice what to wear to bed, but I don't know you well enough to know what you like and what you don't. So tell me, what do you typically wear to bed."

I point to the third drawer. "I usually sleep in one of my nighties."

He quickly finds one of my favorites and turns back to me. "Next time, you don't get out of bed or get dressed without Daddy's permission."

I'm stunned. This is never going to happen again. It's a one-time thing, right? But he makes it seem like it's going to be more than that.

He comes over and pulls the shirt off me. When I try to cover myself, he lets out a growl. "Hands at your sides."

I obey and my nipples harden into points at his stern tone. Luckily, he lowers the nightie over my head quickly.

"Come here, baby girl. Stand up." He grabs my hand and helps me up, then kneels in front of me. It's such a rush when he does that. It makes me feel like such a princess. Yet I have no question in my mind that this man is definitely in charge.

"Hold on to my shoulders and step into your panties."

I do as he says, and he's patient as I step in.

When he pulls them up and settles them over my bottom, he gives me a comforting pat. "Good girl. Do you usually have a bottle at bedtime or suck on a pacifier, or have a sippy cup? I need to know your routine."

I lower my eyes. Telling him something so deeply personal isn't my norm. Kevin never wanted to hear about my routines. He never asked questions. Never wanted to do any extra work.

Jaxon's fingers brush under my chin so I'm forced to look up at him. "Baby girl, I want you to tell me. I'm here to be your Daddy tonight, and I want to take care of you the way you need to be taken care of. Not only do you need this, but I need it too."

His statement hits me deep. I didn't realize he needed this to fulfill his Daddy side too. I guess maybe I was selfish, thinking only of myself. I've always read that some Daddies want or need to have time to be a Daddy, and maybe that's something he needs tonight. It still scares me to tell him the truth. Then again, I am starting my life over here. Maybe I should do things that scare me a little.

"I usually have a bottle with water by the bedside in case I get thirsty, but usually I suck on a pacifier when I go to sleep."

He smiles then brushes a stray hair away from my face. "Thank you, Little bear. I'm going to go get you a bottle and a snack. I want you to try to find a movie while I'm gone. Can you do that for me?"

"Yes. Is there anything you want to watch?"

He shoots me a look. "Baby girl, I want you to find a movie that you want to watch. Find a cartoon movie, something that you enjoy watching in Little Space."

He disappears from the bedroom and Willie follows him. It's adorable how much that dog loves that man. I kind of get it, though. I wonder about wearing a collar and following Jaxon around like a cute little puppy dog. The thought makes me giggle, because that's just ridiculous but might be fun too. Honestly, though, my attraction to him is something that hits me in a way I wasn't expecting.

I decide on *The Secret Life of Pets*. It's one of my favorites, and I think Willie will like it too. Jaxon returns with a plastic plate in his hand and one of my bottles. He had to go through my cupboards to find them. How much of my baby stuff did he find in the process?

It doesn't matter. Tonight's one night. It's never going to happen again, and my only hope is that we can still be friends after this. Although I'm a little disappointed that I'm not going to get to experience his big dick again. That thing was phenomenal.

16

JAXON

Sex with Leah was nothing and everything I expected. I knew it would be great. I didn't know it would be the best sex of my entire life. Her pussy was so tight, it was strangling my cock. I could barely last even a few minutes.

Now, she's in a lavender nightie that has white hearts all over it and a pair of training panties with all sorts of innocent designs on them and she's looking at me like I hung the moon. She pulled her hair free from her ponytail so it hangs around her shoulders in soft waves. Her cheeks are still flushed and those wide eyes of hers make me want to drop to my knees and worship her beauty.

I swallow down all the emotions I'm feeling and sit on the edge of the bed beside her. When I walked out of the bathroom to find her getting dressed, I'd been pissed. While this might only be one night, I didn't just come here to fuck her. I want to Daddy her too. Which is why even though it's nearly one in the morning, I have a plate of snacks in my hand and suggested we watch a movie. If she were my Little girl, I would have her on a strict bedtime schedule, but I want this night to last as long as possible.

"Open," I say as I hold an apple slice up to her mouth.

She obeys. The bear she's clutching looks old and well loved.

"What's his name?"

Her eyebrows pull together as she narrows her eyes at me. "She's a girl."

Whoops. Nothing like offending a Little over a stuffie. "Okay. What's *her* name?"

"Buttercup."

"Cute. She looks well loved. Have you had her a long time?"

Most of her stuffies look old and worn. It makes me want to buy her a few new ones. Something she can snuggle with at night and think of me. Not that she should think about me. After tonight, I'll just be her neighbor again.

"My parents gave me Buttercup in fifth grade. She's my favorite."

Her voice is small and more innocent sounding than normal. I like that all it took was me cleaning her up and getting her ready for bed for her to fall into Little Space. I've gotten a few glimpses of it since we've met but I want to know more about what kinds of things she likes to do, how Little she likes to go, and how often she likes to regress. None of that is my business, though. Doesn't make me want to know any less.

"Where are your parents now?"

Sadness etches her features and I regret asking that question immediately.

"They, uh, they died in a plane crash when I was in my early twenties. My dad had a small plane, and something went wrong while they were in the air."

My chest constricts and a lump forms in my throat. I can't imagine how painful that must be for her. I'm close with my family and the thought of losing them physically hurts.

"I'm so sorry, baby girl. That's terrible."

She blinks several times and gives me a sad smile. "Thanks. I miss them. They gave me most of my stuffies, and that's why they're all so special to me."

"I'm glad you have them. I can tell you love each and every one."

We're both quiet for several minutes until she points to the plate and makes an adorable whining noise.

"Bite?" I ask.

"Yes, please," she replies in a tiny voice.

We eat apples, grapes, and slices of cheese while sitting in companionable silence. *The Secret Life of Pets* is playing on the TV, and I wonder if it's her favorite. Something inside me wants to know what all of her favorites are.

This woman is doing something to me I haven't felt in a long time. A pull I can't resist. Maybe it's because she's vulnerable and alone, so I feel extra protective of her. There's no doubt in my mind that she's a strong woman, but she could still use someone to look out for her. I can't give her anything more than my friendship. I can look out for her as a friend. Keep my distance but at the same time, make sure she's not climbing on shit or doing dangerous things.

"Is this your favorite movie?" I finally ask.

A smile spreads on her face making her dimples appear. "No. I mean, I like it, but it's not my favorite. I thought Willie would enjoy it."

At his name, my dog lifts his head and lets out a single bark of agreement before he sighs and goes back to sleep. A warm feeling fills my chest. She chose the movie because she thought he would enjoy it. This is bad. So damn bad. Walking away from her tomorrow is going to be torture.

When we finish eating, I sit on her bed with my back against the headboard and pull the blankets over my legs. "Come here, baby girl."

She looks at me with uncertainty as I hold my arms out for her. After hesitating for a second, she crawls over and lets me pull her onto my lap to cradle her against my chest. I refuse to think about how right this feels. How perfectly her body fits against mine. I'm just going to enjoy tonight with her. If I'm totally honest, it's been one of the best nights of my life.

"Where's your pacifier, Little bear?"

I feel her go stiff, but she quickly relaxes before she points to the top drawer of her nightstand. Without asking, I reach over and open it. When I look over, I notice a couple of vibrators along with a handful of pacifiers. I wonder how often she uses those toys and what she thinks about when she does. Has she ever fantasized about me while getting herself off? The thought makes my cock twitch. Instead of asking, I grab the pacifier I saw on top of the nightstand before and close the drawer. I hold the nipple up to her lips and press gently. I'm pleased when she obediently opens her mouth.

While we watch the movie, my mind wanders. So many questions and what ifs. What if I took a chance with her? Would she be interested? What if we did a friends with benefits situation? Am I falling for her?

Her body eventually goes slack against mine and her breathing evens out. Instead of turning off the movie right away, I sit and watch her sleep as she suckles on her pacifier. There are so many questions I don't know the answer to. One thing I do know is this: I don't remember the last time I felt this peaceful and that scares the hell out of me.

WAKING up with Leah's warm body pressed against mine is wonderful torture. I slept better than I've slept in years. My cock is hard as a rock for her, but after round two in the middle of the night, I worry about her being sore, so I'll have to ignore it. As much as I love the thought of her being a bit achy so she's forced to think about me every time she moves today, I don't want to cause her any real pain.

As carefully as possible, I unfold myself from her warmth and reluctantly slide out of bed. I could stay wrapped up with her under the covers all day and be perfectly content. That isn't an option, though, so I pay a visit to the bathroom before heading to the kitchen to start a pot of coffee for us. Willie trots behind me and I let him out to do his morning business then sit on the couch with a steaming black cup of happiness.

Her soft footsteps padding down the hall make me rise and go to the kitchen to pour her a cup of coffee. Her sleepy smile when she approaches hits me right in the gut. Even though she doesn't have her pacifier in, she still looks so Little and perfectly innocent.

"Morning, Little bear. Do you take cream?"

Her eyes sparkle as she holds out her cup for me to give her some French vanilla creamer.

"More," she says when I stop pouring.

With a raised eyebrow, I add a bit more.

"More," she whines.

"Baby, you have more creamer than coffee in there."

Her bottom lip pops out. "Please?"

I shake my head and pour another splash into her cup. She sighs but I can see her lips pulling back into a smile as she goes to take her first sip.

"Mmm. Yummy."

Goddamn. Her little noises of appreciation make my cock thicken. I need to get out of here before I start thinking shit I have no business thinking. Like long term commitment.

I set my mug down with a thud that startles her. "We need to go get your car from the bar."

"I can walk there and pick it up later."

Annoyance fills me. Why does this woman always have to argue with me when I offer to help? "I'm driving you and that's final. Go get dressed."

She rolls her eyes but turns around and takes her coffee back to her room with her. Willie follows and I feel a bit betrayed by my own dog. A few minutes later, she returns wearing a pair of leggings and a hoodie. The sweatshirt is so big it makes me wonder if it was her ex's. I hate the idea of her wearing another man's clothes. Yet another reason why I need to get the fuck out of here and away from her. I can't think straight when we're together.

"Let's go," she murmurs before she gulps down a final sip of coffee.

The drive to the bar is quiet and when she turns to get out of my truck, I grab her wrist. "Hey."

She pauses, and I don't like her look of uncertainty. I want to soothe whatever doubt she's feeling.

"Last night was really amazing. Thank you for trusting me. You're a beautiful woman and a very special Little girl."

Relief floods me when she gives me a full-wattage smile.

"Thank you. You're a really good Daddy. I had the best time."

Even though I know I shouldn't, I can't resist pulling her to me. We stare at each other for a long moment before I press my lips to hers. It's not hard and possessive like it was last night. This kiss is soft and intimate.

When I pull back, I rest my forehead on hers. "What are you doing today?"

"Natalie, Bree, and Greer are coming over for a girls' day. We're going to watch movies and stuff."

I'm glad she's making new friends. "Sounds fun. Be a good girl. I have a feeling the four of you together might be trouble waiting to happen."

She giggles and opens the passenger door. "Getting into trouble is the best kind of fun. Have a good day, Jaxon."

"You too, Little bear. I'll see you."

"See you." And with that, she closes me into the cab of my truck, and I already miss her.

Shit.

I'm so fucking screwed.

17

LEAH

After Jaxon drops me off at the bar, I head to the grocery store to get snacks. For our girls' day, Bree is bringing wine, and I said that I would get the makings for a charcuterie board AKA a Littles Lunchable. We plan on watching movies and talking. I'm sort of glad that Jaxon limited me to only two drinks last night, because otherwise I'd probably be feeling like crap today. My body's sore, but in the best way possible.

Not that I would ever tell him, but I'm already aching for his touch again. Last night was the best night I've had in my entire life. It's amazing how one person and one night can make you feel like you're the most precious, amazing thing in the world. I've never felt as beautiful as I did when he was touching me.

I thought things would be awkward this morning and I'm so glad they weren't. He was just as sweet as he was last night. When he left me with the reminder to be a good girl with my friends, I wanted to stick my tongue out at him and remind him he's not the boss of me. The look that he shot me told me he knew exactly what I was thinking. It was fun and lighthearted. Something that I'm not used to with Jaxon. It was nice to get a glimpse of it.

He's actually a really fun guy when he lets go enough to relax. Not sure why it's so hard for him or why he's so closed off. I have a feeling it has to do with his ex-wife. She really did a number on him. I should ask my friends what they know about it. Then again, that feels like it would be a betrayal to Jaxon. Small-town gossip isn't something I want to get involved in. If he wants me to know more than what he already told me, he'll share when he's ready.

After getting all the makings for our Littles Lunchable, I head back to my house and start putting it together. Once everything looks perfect on the tray, I put it in the refrigerator and go take a shower. It feels so good to have the hot water pound all my achy muscles. When I start thinking about Jaxon, naked and hovering over me with his cock buried deep in my pussy, my hand trails down the front of my stomach.

I circle my fingers around my clit while I continue to think about every single thing we did last night. How he ate me from behind, and how he woke me up in the middle of the night to fuck me again, pulling my training panties down to my thighs before he thrust deep into me. It was an amazing feeling. He pushed my pacifier back in and we fell right to sleep, tangled together, so peaceful and quiet.

After my shower, I dry my hair and put on a pair of soft pink leggings and a matching oversized knit sweater. The four of us decided that we're probably going to be in Little Space today, so we might as well be comfortable. Instead of wearing training panties, though, I'm wearing just a normal pair of briefs. White with lace trim. Cotton, of course. There's something about cotton that always makes me feel so small and innocent.

Natalie is the first one to arrive. Then Greer, then Bree.

They squeal excitedly as soon as they walk in the door, wanting to know the details of my sexual escapades. I can't help but laugh right along with them. I shouldn't be giving details of our hot night, but at the same time, Jaxon knew they were coming over today. Of course he would know that women talk and that I'm going to tell my friends. It was obvious to everyone that we went home together so it's not like it's some big secret. Besides, the girls have promised me total secrecy within our friendship circle and even though I haven't known them for very long, I do trust them.

"So, tell us everything," Bree insists.

I'm on the couch with Natalie at the opposite end, Bree is on the chair to the right, and Greer is curled up with a bunch of throw pillows on the floor. We already put in our first movie, but we haven't started on the food and drinks yet.

"What am I supposed to say? We had a good time."

A pillow gets tossed at me.

"Oh, come on. There has got to be more to the story than that," Greer says.

I'm grinning from ear to ear like a damn fool. They know a lot more went down than just a good time. And it's true. It was an amazing time. The best sex I've ever had in my life.

"Is he totally hung?" Natalie asks.

We burst out in giggles, and I slap my hand over my mouth as I nod. They erupt into loud squeals.

"Hung is an understatement. I never understood the saying 'hung like a horse.' I do now. I should have expected it since Jaxon is a big guy, but I hadn't quite expected *that*. Not that I'm complaining." My cheeks are flaming hot and I can't look any of them directly in the eye.

"Oh my God. I knew it. I just knew it. Jaxon has always had that big dick energy," Greer says.

We laugh uncontrollably. They continue to ask a million questions, and I answer them the best I can without feeling like I'm giving them all the intimate details of our night together. Some of it I want to keep for me. I do tell them about how he made me food and hand fed me, then held me in his arms while we watched a movie. It was so sweet. One of the best feelings ever. He was truly being a Daddy.

When they finally get all the juicy details and they're satisfied with my answers, we grab our food and pour our glasses of wine.

"So what's going on between you and Austin?" I ask Greer.

Her cheeks turn bright red and she takes a big gulp of wine then waves her hand in the air dismissively. "Oh, nothing. Austin is my brother's best friend. I've known him forever. He's a bossy pain in the ass."

I raise an eyebrow and meet Bree's gaze. She looks like she doesn't believe Greer either.

"I don't get the impression it's nothing based on the way he looks at you," Natalie says.

Greer rolls her eyes. "He looks at me like I'm an annoying bug he can't squash. There's nothing going on between me and Austin."

I'm still not convinced but I don't push it. Instead, we start watching the movie.

My phone vibrates about halfway through. Jaxon's name is on the screen. A grin spreads on my face and all the girls start squealing.

"Is that Jaxon?" Natalie asks.

I turn bright red as I open the message and they all shriek.

> Jaxon: I hope you're all being good girls. And if you're drinking, I hope you're eating too.

I lick my lips.

Jaxon

> Leah: No, we're just drinking straight from the bottles and having a good time.

Three dots appear instantly.

> Jaxon: Little bear.

It makes me laugh. I love the nickname he's given me.

> Leah: We are eating.

I take a picture of the charcuterie board and send it to him.

> Jaxon: Good girl. Have fun.

"Oh, my god, you guys, look at her face. She's freaking glowing," Greer says.

Natalie and Bree bob their heads.

"So, when are you guys going to hook up again?" Bree asks.

I wave them off. "We're not. It was a one-time thing. We're just going to be friends or neighbors or whatever."

They all roll their eyes at the same time.

"Uh huh. Okay. Must be nice to be in denial," Greer replies.

I narrow my eyes. "Says the one who insists there's nothing between her and her brother's best friend."

Greer sticks her tongue out at me, and we all burst out into a fit of giggles.

It warms me inside to know he's checking on me, but he's also telling me to have fun with my friends. It's not something I'm used to. Anytime I hung out with friends when I was with Kevin, he refused to leave me alone with them. He said it was because he wanted to spend time with me, but I know better now. He didn't trust me.

The rest of the day goes by, and I don't hear from Jaxon. To say I'm disappointed is an understatement, but at the same time, I'm kind of surprised that he messaged me today at all. I suppose we're going to be friends now. It's hard, though, because even though he and I have only known each other for a couple of weeks, I know deep down that he's a good man. He's different than what I initially thought.

By the time our girls' day ends, we've all been laughing so hard our cheeks hurt. I feel like I found my girl gang. We even played Barbies for a while. I worried it would be awkward, but nothing about our friendship feels weird.

They all leave, and I'm floating around the house, feeling a natural high. Making friends, getting fucked, being taking care of like a precious Little girl. It does wonders for a woman. I finally feel like I found my place in the world. I fit in here. Even though things with Jaxon and I won't go any further, it still feels good to be wanted and desired by someone I find just as sexy.

I SPEND my Monday putting together floral arrangements and fulfilling orders. I love my job and I love flowers. I'm blessed to have found this shop right when they were looking for a lead florist. Since I'd worked as a florist in Portland, Blossom and Bloom hired me on the spot and allowed me time to find a house and move before starting.

When I get home and see his truck in his driveway, I push away the twinge of sadness I feel. I want to go over there and ask him how his day was. I want to pet Willie then snuggle on Jaxon's lap while he watches football or whatever he does on Monday nights.

Instead, I go into my house and spend the evening doing

more unpacking and decorating. When I get to the box of framed photos, I get a little emotional as I pull out the photos of my parents. Seeing their faces soothes me, and I find the perfect shelves to set them on so they're surrounding me in the house. It's starting to feel like a home. There's still a lot of work to be done, but it's become my safe space. Something I haven't had in way too long.

I go to bed around ten, only to be woken up at two in the morning with painful cramps, laying on blood soaked sheets. This is one of those things that makes me hate myself. Why do I have to be broken? I never know when I'm going to get my damn period. It just comes out of the blue, and it's painful and heavy and I never know if it's going to last two days or two weeks.

It's been two months since my last one. You'd think after all these years, I'd be used to this kind of thing. But every time, I feel worse about myself. Maybe it's the hormones. Or maybe waking up in such a mess just makes me emotional.

After I take a shower and get myself cleaned up, I put on one of those ridiculously large maxi pads. I might as well just wear a diaper, but I don't have the energy to go find one in my stash of Little items.

Once I'm in a pair of comfy pajamas, I pull my bedding off. After this many years of waking up in bloody messes, I've learned to have a waterproof mattress protector. I'm especially thankful for it right now. After throwing everything in the wash, I remake my bed. The cramps are already in full force, and I'm practically in tears curling into myself as each one hits. I already know I'm not going to be able to go to work in the morning. I down a couple ibuprofen with the water that's in my bottle, then slide my pacifier between my lips.

Hopefully the medicine starts working soon. It's not going to help enough, but it'll take the edge off and that's honestly all I really need. I can handle cramps, but what I'm experiencing now is so painful, I feel like vomiting.

I think it's after four when I finally fall asleep. My alarm goes off at six, and I send a text to my boss. I'd informed her of my condition when she hired me. Thankfully, she understands. Her daughter has PCOS too and has had painful periods all her life.

After she tells me to take as many days as I need, I spend the next several hours in agonizing pain trying to doze off again. Unfortunately, with the cramps, nausea, my aching lower back, and messy emotions, I can't fall asleep.

At one point I'm in tears and consider getting in the bathtub to soak, but I've done that before and sitting in your own pool of blood isn't a lot of fun. I'm not in the mafia after all. Blood baths aren't really my thing. So, I decide against it.

I don't know how long I lie there, but I start to drift to sleep only to be woken by someone pounding at my front door. I have no idea who it could be and honestly getting up is extremely unappealing. For all I know, one of my old neighbors could have an emergency. With a whimper, I drag myself out of bed, nearly doubling over in pain as I make my way to the front door. When I open it, all the air rushes from my lungs as Jaxon stares down at me with worry.

"Jaxon?"

He steps into the house and closes the door behind him, then turns to me again. "I stopped by your work and your boss said you were home sick today. You're in pain. What's wrong, baby?"

I rub my hand over my face, trying to keep the tears that are burning the backs of my eyes at bay. "It's just my period. I'm fine."

"Yeah, that's a lie and we'll talk about that later," he says as he scoops me off my feet and makes his way to my bedroom.

Jaxon

Afraid he might drop me I wrap my arms around his neck to hold on. "What are you doing?"

He sets me on the bed and pulls the blankets up over me. "Taking care of you. I read that people with PCOS have really painful and heavy periods. I'll be right back."

Before I can get my next question out, he disappears. A minute later, he returns with a bag in one hand and Willie trotting behind him. I stare at him, unsure what the hell is going on.

"Willie, up," he commands.

The dog jumps onto my bed, and Jaxon tells him to lie down. He immediately curls up next to me, the warmth of his furry body soothing some of my achiness. I stroke his fur as I watch Jaxon pull stuff from the bag.

"What is all that?"

He shrugs. "A heating pad, liquid pain killer, a natural pain relief cream, chocolate, diapers, bath salts, and electrolyte drinks."

My eyes bug out. "What?"

I don't even know what's happening right now. Maybe I'm in so much pain that I'm delirious and he's not really here.

"I told you, I did some reading about PCOS. These are what they suggested to help with painful and heavy periods. Well, except the diapers. I figured a diaper would be better for you so you don't have to get up to change your pad and I can just change you."

Using my fists, I rub my eyes and blink several times, confident that I'm hallucinating. Did he really just say all that? This isn't real. It's a dream. Maybe the ibuprofen I took got mixed up with some kind of other drug and I'm actually high right now.

A cramp hits me, and I curl into myself with a groan. No, this is definitely real. If I were high or hallucinating, I wouldn't feel this much pain.

Jaxon puts his hand on my lower back and starts massaging me while I wait for the pain to pass.

When it does, I uncurl and look up at him with watery eyes. "Why are you here?"

"It's simple, Little bear. We're friends, but today you need a Daddy to take care of you. Your only job right now is to let me."

18

JAXON

She's in so much pain. It's written all over her face. She's paler than I've ever seen her, and the way she keeps curling into herself kills me. I hate this for her.

"All right, baby, I'm going to go fill your bottle with an electrolyte drink and get you something to eat to take with your medication."

She groans. "I don't think I can keep anything down."

I swipe my hand over her clammy forehead. "I know you don't feel well, baby, but I need you to try and do it for me, okay? I have something you might be able to eat."

She whimpers and hugs her tummy. "Okay."

"I'm gonna go grab it, and I'll be right back. Willie, stay."

All the spark and fight is gone from her eyes, replaced with pure agony. When I went to Blossom and Bloom, her boss told me she was out sick. I had a feeling it was probably something to do with her period. She had told me that they were so painful she had to miss work sometimes. After she told me all that, I researched PCOS and I'm glad I did. While I can't take the pain away, I at least know some things to do for her that will help manage it.

I grab several jars of pureed vegetables and applesauce from my pantry. I had picked them up at the grocery store the last time I was there because the label made me think of her. It's ridiculous that I was thinking of her when I was grocery shopping, but this sweet little girl hasn't left my mind since I met her, and I don't think she'll leave that space any time soon.

She's had it too rough the past several years. I'm already positive that asshole ex never took care of her when she was hurting. I want to do what I can to make it better for her. She's more than just a neighbor to me. I don't want to think about what that means because honestly, I don't know how to define what we are.

When I get back to her house, I hear movement in her room so I head directly back there to check on her. She's breathing heavily as she tries to stand.

"What are you doing, Little bear?"

"I need to go to the bathroom."

I scoop her off her feet, then carry her into the bathroom, not setting her down until we reach the toilet.

She stares up at me expectantly. "I need privacy, Jaxon."

I shake my head. "I don't want to leave you alone. You're weak and you're hurting. Let me help you."

Her face twists into a feisty scowl, her eyes narrowed at me. "I can go potty by myself."

I want to demand that she let me stay, but we don't know each other well enough for that yet, and we're not in any kind of dynamic, so I give her a slight nod. "I'll be right outside the door if you need anything, just call out, okay? Daddy's here to take care of you."

I don't know why I called myself Daddy. We're not together and my night of being her Daddy is over, but it's something I feel deep within me and I'm not going to analyze it to death right now.

Jaxon

"Thank you, Daddy," she whispers as I make my way out of the bathroom.

My heart swells and I feel like I'm on top of the world. I pull on the bathroom door but don't close it all the way. I want to be close in case she calls out.

I hear her start to pee, then several movements and the rustling sound of what I assume is probably her changing her pad. Once she's done in there, I'm going to try and talk her into letting me diaper her. I hate the fact that it's so painful for her to get out of bed. It would be better if I could just clean her up and change her when needed. As soon as I hear the toilet flush, I walk back in.

"Jaxon!"

"What? I heard the toilet flush. I came to help you. I don't want you walking back to your bed by yourself."

She sighs and hobbles over to the sink to wash her hands, confusion written all over her features. "I don't understand what you're doing here. Aren't you supposed to be at work? Why did you even go by Blossom and Bloom in the first place?"

I step behind her at the sink, reach my arms over hers and pump some foamy soap into my palm before I start scrubbing her hands with mine.

"I was at the police station. My friend Asher—one of the ones at the bar the other night—is a police officer, and I went to go get his house key because I'm starting a renovation project for him. I was right there, so I stopped by to say hi, but your boss said that you were out sick. That's why I'm here."

Her wide eyes stare at me in the mirror. "But you have work to do. I'm okay. I can take care of myself."

It takes everything in me not to growl at her. I want to pop her on her bottom and remind her that she doesn't have to do everything by herself. Instead, I lower my head and press a gentle kiss to her temple.

"I know you can do it by yourself, but you don't have to. And I want to be here. I own the company. Silas is my head foreman. I don't have to be there every day, so I'm going to be here for the rest of the day and you're going to let me take care of you, okay?"

She leans back into my chest and sighs. "Okay."

I'm glad she's not arguing with me because she wouldn't win. I'm going to be here whether she likes it or not. As soon as her hands are dry, I pick her up and carry her back into her room, setting her gently on the bed.

"I'm gonna change you into a diaper so you don't have to get out of bed from now on."

Her eyes widen and she shakes her head so hard I'm surprised it doesn't snap right off. "No, I don't want a diaper on. I don't want you to have to see any of that."

I tilt my head and pin her with my gaze. "Do you think I've never seen blood before, baby?"

She's still shaking her head. "I'm sure you have, but not like this. My periods are really heavy when I have them and I just can't, Jaxon. I'm not ready for that."

I let out a deep, unhappy sigh, but I don't argue with her because if it's a limit for her, I'm not going to push it. For now, I'll just make sure that I carry her to and from the bathroom for the rest of the day.

Once she's covered up again, I grab Buttercup and press the bear into her arms.

"I brought some jars of pureed food. One is applesauce and the other is apples, sweet potatoes, and carrots. At least it's some kind of nutrition and it will help the pain medicine work better. Can you try and eat for me?"

She makes a face that I can't quite distinguish. Jealousy maybe? "You have baby food at your house?"

I chuckle. "I didn't until I met this sweet Little girl that lives next door to me. When I saw them at the store, they

Jaxon

made me think of her because the jar has little bears on the front."

The smile that she gives me is so worth buying the food. She takes one of the jars from me to look at the label with the bear on it while I measure out some liquid painkiller.

"Open," I instruct.

She eyes the tiny cup filled with purple liquid then opens her lips for me to pour it into her mouth. After she swallows, she hums a sound of approval that makes me chuckle.

"Good girl. Drink some of your bottle. The electrolytes will help with the cramps."

After going to the kitchen to find a plastic baby spoon, I sit on the edge of the bed next to her. Willie is still curled up on the other side.

"What flavor do you want first?"

"Applesauce, please."

We sit in silence as I start to feed her. I have no idea what this food might taste like but she continues to take spoonful's of the applesauce so it can't be too bad.

"How do you know electrolytes help with cramps?" she asks.

I shrug. "I did some research on PCOS and ways to help alleviate painful period symptoms."

Her mouth falls open as she stares at me in shock. I slide the spoon between her lips.

"You really looked up information on it?"

"Yeah. I mean, it affects you, so I wanted to know more about it. Chocolate helps too. The topical lotion is good for helping lower back pain. I'll rub some on you when you're done eating."

Tears well in her eyes. "You...Jaxon... What? I don't understand what's happening here."

Using my thumb, I brush her falling tears. Shit. I didn't mean to make her cry.

"I'm not sure either, Little bear. I just know I care about you."

She sniffles and leans her head forward until it's resting on my bicep. "Thank you, Daddy."

I've never loved being called that as much as I do right now. It's a terrifying feeling. One I'm not sure how to handle. It doesn't matter right now, though. She needs to be taken care of today so I'm going to have to examine my feelings for her later.

When she's eaten two jars of food, I'm satisfied, so I get out the heating pad and plug it in.

"Roll over onto your tummy. Let Daddy rub some lotion on your back."

Her cheeks turn pink but she does what I ask and when I lift up the back of her nightie, her breath hitches. Mine does too and my cock aches in my jeans. I don't think I'll ever look at her bottom and not get hard.

As soon as I'm done, she lets me slide the heating pad under her lower tummy.

"Do you need to go potty again before you go to sleep?"

She nibbles on her bottom lip and looks over at me. "I'm okay."

I kick my boots off before climbing into bed next to her.

"What are you doing?" she asks.

"I'm going to lie with you and rub your back. I want you to close your eyes and rest."

Without asking, I grab a pacifier from her nightstand and push it gently between her lips. I roll onto my side to face her and start rubbing circles on her lower back. I'm pleased when her eyes flutter closed, and her delicate fingers move to my chest as though she's using me instead of one of her stuffies for comfort.

It only takes a few minutes before her breathing evens out and she's deep asleep next to me. I can't help but wonder what it would be like if this were my life and the thought soothes me more than it scares me. I'm falling for Leah Day. I just don't know if I'd survive it if she ever hurt me. My feelings for her are already stronger than anything I ever felt for my ex. This sweet, strong woman next to me has the power to destroy me and I don't think that's a chance I can take.

19

LEAH

I wake up feeling so warm. Like I have a thick blanket wrapped around me. My cramps aren't nearly as intense as they were before. When I open my eyes, I'm not alone. I'm facing Jaxon. And Willie's right behind me curled up against my back.

I can't believe he researched PCOS just because he cares about me. Then came to my house to take care of me when I couldn't do it myself.

His eyes are closed, and he looks so peaceful. It's the first time I can stare at his features without him knowing. He has one arm wrapped around me, and the other is under my shoulder.

I have no idea how long I've been sleeping. Has he stayed with me the entire time? I remember him getting into bed and rubbing my back. The man offered to diaper me, for goodness sake. I'm glad I was at least coherent enough to tell him no, because if he had to deal with the homicide scene in my panties, he'd never speak to me again.

The reminder that I need to get up and go to the bathroom makes me stir and try to slide out from between the two warm bodies sandwiching me. As soon as I move, Jaxon's eyes open.

"Hey, Little bear. How are you feeling?"

I nuzzle my face into his chest for a brief moment. "I feel so much better. Thank you. I hadn't been able to sleep the night before, and the ibuprofen I'd taken hadn't done anything. Whatever you gave me, it worked."

He strokes my hair. "I gave you ibuprofen too, baby. But I also gave you food with it, and that's probably why it helped. You're not supposed to take it on an empty stomach. I'm glad you're feeling better. Do you need to go potty?"

"Yes, please. I was trying to get up without waking you."

He rises, then turns and scoops me up.

I wiggle in his arms. "Jaxon, you've got to stop picking me up."

He lets out a growl. "Why? I like carrying you."

This man is exasperating sometimes. "Because I'm too heavy and if you keep carrying me, you're going to have a bad back."

He narrows his eyes. "That's two."

My eyebrows shoot up in confusion. "That's two what?"

"That's one spanking you're going to get for putting yourself down and you earned yourself another one earlier when you lied to me about being fine. You're not heavy. You're healthy and I'm going to remind you of that with a warm bottom later. I won't spank you while you're not feeling well, but once you're better, we're gonna have a chat about it with you face down over my lap."

A shiver runs through me at the thought of Jaxon spanking me. I'm intrigued about being disciplined, and I want to know what that might feel like, but also, I'm not so sure I want to experience his huge hands on my bottom for a true spanking.

"I wasn't putting myself down. I was just stating the obvious," I argue.

Jaxon

His lips thin as he shoots me a glare. "No, you were putting yourself down. I don't want to hear you speak like that again."

I sigh and rest my head against his chest, deciding not to argue. The man is as stubborn as a goat, so I won't win anyway.

He sets me down in front of the toilet. "I'll be right outside if you need me."

I quickly do my business, thankful that I didn't bleed through my pad. I actually got some good sleep and even though I'm still having cramps, they're nothing like they were earlier. As soon as I'm finished, I wash my hands and, when I open the door, he's standing right on the other side waiting for me.

"Are you hungry?"

I shrug. "I think I could eat something. My mouth is dry. I need to get something to drink."

He smiles and goes to my nightstand to grab my bottle. My face heats when he holds the nipple up to my mouth. "Open."

I do as he says and take several long pulls from the bottle of the sweet electrolyte juice he brought. When I'm done, he grabs my hand. "Come on. I want you to sit on the couch with the heating pad on your back while I find us something to eat. I have some chocolate for you too."

I'm still so confused as to why this man is here. Why did he show up when he found out I was sick? Why did he research PCOS? Why does he even care? He made it clear we're just neighbors and friends. That's something a Daddy would do. Before I can ask any of those questions, he grabs the heating pad and leads me out to the living room.

Once he gets it plugged in and set on the couch, he waits for me to sit and then puts a blanket over me.

He hands me my bottle. "I want you to drink the rest of this while I make some food."

There's no room for argument in his tone so I start to drink as he flips on the TV and surfs until he finds a cartoon channel. He's so incredibly thoughtful. Completely different than what I first thought of him. I like Jaxon Sawyer. More than as a friend. I'm so afraid that I'm going to get my heart broken. He's made it clear he'll never have another relationship again. I respect that. I'm probably not ready for a relationship either. Staying friends is probably the best option. It just feels like there's so much more to us than that.

The heating pad warms me, and I relax into the cushions. I've never had someone take care of me when I've had one of my bad periods. Kevin would have avoided me at all costs. He would even go sleep in the other room just so that he didn't have to deal with me possibly waking him up in the middle of the night because I leaked blood. Meanwhile, Jaxon just ran right into the fire with all the tools he needed to help me through it, not caring if he got blood on his hands.

Suddenly, I feel like I've been hit by a ton of bricks because I'm pretty sure I'm in love with my neighbor. Crap. This is bad. So, so bad.

The house is filling with the delicious smells of butter and garlic. I have no idea what he's cooking, but I'm practically drooling for it. I force myself to be a good girl and drink the bottle like he told me to. When he sits down next to me with a plate in hand, he gives me a full-wattage Jaxon Sawyer smile that melts my panties.

"Good girl drinking all of that. I'll give you a reward for obeying Daddy after we eat."

My ears perk up over the reward, but also hearing him call himself Daddy. I swear he was made for this lifestyle. I wish he wanted something more with me. Never have I felt the feelings for a man that I feel toward him.

I'm starting to realize I don't even think I was ever in love with Kevin. I was attracted to the picture he painted for me. The one that never actually came to fruition because after we got married, he changed and the things he said he wanted were different. There's no doubt in my mind that with Jaxon, what you see is what you get.

"Mmm, that smells so yummy." He made grilled cheese and tomato soup, one of my favorite meals when I'm not feeling well.

He picks up a piece of the sandwich and holds it to my mouth. "Yeah, well, when I'm sick, this is what makes me feel better."

A smile spreads as I chew my bite and let out a little moan of approval. "This is so good. What did you do different?"

"I use garlic butter on the bread before I toast it and then add another layer of butter halfway through."

It takes everything in me not to start calculating the calorie count of all that butter. Jaxon says he likes me as I am so that's good enough for me. Besides, I'm pretty sure I burned at least three million calories during our wild sex adventures the other night.

"You really didn't have to come here today, you know."

A scowl forms on his face and he glares at me, making me shrink back a little.

"I know I didn't have to, Leah. I wanted to. I was worried about you, and even though I know you're strong enough to do all this shit by yourself, you shouldn't have to. You were in so much pain you could barely walk. From now on, I want a text every time you start your period so I can come take care of you in case it gets bad. End of discussion."

Seriously? Heat rises to my cheeks, and I have half a mind to argue, curse him out, and then boot him out of my house. The problem with that is I'm pretty sure he wouldn't leave if I told him to, and also, I'm totally melting inside.

"You're a stubborn man, you know. Totally impossible," I mumble.

He holds the sandwich up to my mouth again. "I know."

Before I take a bite, I look him directly in the eye. "Thank you. What you did today was the nicest thing anyone has ever done for me."

Every inch of him tenses as he stares at me silently, and I'm worried I said something to upset him. When I open my mouth to apologize, I'm stopped when his lips land on mine. The plate clatters as he sets it on the coffee table and moves both of his hands to cup my face as he kisses me deeply and thoroughly. It isn't until I remember I haven't brushed my teeth in over twenty four hours that I pull away.

"I need to brush my teeth," I squeak as I try to get up.

He grabs my wrist and pulls me down onto his lap. "You don't need to brush your teeth. You need to sit on Daddy's lap and let me finish feeding you. After that, you can take a shower and brush your teeth. Then, we're going to spend the rest of the day watching movies while I take care of you."

"Do I get a say in any of this?"

"Nope. The only way you get a say is if you say red. Would you like to say red?"

I don't need to think about it. I shake my head. His eyes crinkle in the corners as he gives me a pleased smile and picks up the plate of food again.

He feeds me the sandwich and then the soup, not letting me do any of it by myself. I feel Little and cherished and incredibly special. This giant growly man has wrapped his big bear hands around my heart, and I know I will never be the same again because of him. It scares the life out of me.

"Would you prefer a bath or shower?" he asks.

I don't want to explain my disinterest in taking a blood-bath, so I choose shower. He puts our plates in the sink then comes back and scoops me off my feet. I wiggle against his hold because he's the first man to ever carry me and my anxiety spikes every time he does it. Whether he agrees or not, I'm much too heavy to be carried.

"I can hear those negative thoughts in your head and

unless you want me to add a third spanking to your punishment, I suggest you stop. You're perfect just as you are, Little bear."

When I let out a loud sigh, he shoots me a stern look. I give him a wide, innocent smile in return that makes him roll his eyes and chuckle.

"Such a brat."

"But I'm fun, at least."

He's full on smiling now. "Yes, you are a lot of fun. Even if most of my gray hairs are from you."

I run my fingers through his beard. "Yeah, but you look pretty sexy with that gray."

His fingers dig into my flesh, and he lets out a quiet growl. When he sets me on my feet in the bathroom, I notice the outline of his erection in his jeans. Why do I have to be on my stupid period?

"You have two minutes to go potty and dispose of your pad without me in here and then I'm coming back in."

He leaves the bathroom before I can ask why he would be back in. I stare at the closed door in shocked silence before I realize I'm running out of time, so I hustle to the toilet. That man is too bossy for his own good. And there must be something wrong with me that I love it so much.

As soon as I'm finished, he walks in like he owns the place and pulls his shirt up and over his head. My eyes widen as I take in all his thick muscles and tattoos. The man is fine with a capital F.

"What are you doing?" I finally find the words to ask.

"We're taking a shower."

"What? Why? I can take a shower by myself."

He stalks toward me and cups my chin. "Yes, but Daddy wants to take a shower with you. Now, arms up."

I'm so stunned that I immediately obey and when he pulls my nightie over my head, leaving me in just a pair of panties, I let out a squeak and try to cover myself.

"Arms at your sides," he barks.

It takes all the courage I can muster to lower my arms from my saggy boobs and place them at my sides. His gaze roams over me and he licks his lips in appreciation.

When he starts unbuckling his belt, I can't stop my own eyes from roaming over him. His cock springs out of his underwear as he pulls them down and I want to drop to my knees and taste it. Before I get the chance, he moves to the shower and turns it on then comes to me and removes my panties.

"In you go," he says as he lifts me by the hips and sets me in the tub.

He shuts the glass door and disappears from the bathroom for just a few seconds before he returns with something in his hand. He sets the item up on the railing so I can't see it and then moves his hands to my hair.

The next few minutes are spent with him shampooing and conditioning my hair then washing my entire body. When I tried to insist I could do it myself, he smacked my bottom. It was only once but it was sharp enough to get my attention and stop me from arguing with him. I've never had a man shower with me before let alone take care of me in such an intimate way. It's sexy and I'm practically panting by the time he's done.

"Turn around and face me."

As soon as I obey, something touches my clit and starts to vibrate. I jolt.

"Shh. Relax, baby. This is your reward for being such a good girl. It will help you feel better."

I'm so confused. And oh, my God, he's touching me down there. I start to push his hand away.

"Jaxon, no. I'm on my period. It's gross."

He raises an eyebrow. "There is nothing gross down there whether you're on your period or not. Besides, we're in the shower. A few orgasms will make you feel so much better."

I'm left gaping up at him as he returns the vibrating toy to my clit. Within seconds, I'm moaning and clawing at his biceps for balance. He snakes his free arm around my lower back and pulls me against him, his hard erection pressing to my tummy. I reach for it, but he stops me.

"Ignore my cock. This is about you, baby. I'm here to make you feel good."

I pop my bottom lip out in a pout as I look up at him. "But that makes me feel good."

His smile is cocky as he stares at me, still circling my clit with the toy. "Daddy's cock makes you feel good, baby? You like when I fuck you hard and deep while spanking your lush bottom?"

A shiver runs through me as I moan and bob my head. "Yes. Oh, shit."

He dips his head down and takes one of my nipples between his lips.

Sucking.

Nibbling.

"Daddy. Oh! Oh! Please!"

"Please, what, baby? Please let you come? Do you want to show Daddy what a perfect Little girl you are and come for me? Is that what you want?"

I throw my head back and cry out as my legs start to tremble. "Yes! Please, I need to…I…Oh, fuck!"

My climax hits me so hard my knees give out and he has to hold me up as I shake and scream while he keeps the toy trained on my clit.

"That's a good girl. Yes, come for Daddy, baby. You're so fucking beautiful like this," he murmurs against my ear.

When I start to settle, I expect him to pull the toy away, but he doesn't. Instead, he turns it to another speed and keeps teasing.

"Daddy," I whimper.

"I want you to come again, baby. It will make you feel better."

I shake my head. "I can't. I...I want you."

His eyes darken and his face has pure possessiveness written all over it. "You want Daddy to bend you over in this shower and fuck your tight little pussy?"

"Yes!" I cry out. "Wait, no. Never mind."

He shakes his head. "Nope. You already said yes."

"I'm on my period, Jaxon."

One of his hands lands on my ass with a hard smack. "*Daddy*. And I don't give a fuck if you're on your period. If it will make you feel good, we're doing it."

I shake my head because it's wrong. It's gross and dirty and just because I want it doesn't mean he should give it to me.

Before I can argue, he spins me around and places my hands on the shower wall then grabs my hips with force and yanks them back until my bottom meets his erection.

"You're going to learn that Daddy doesn't give a fuck about a little blood. Does it seem like it's turning me off right now, Little bear?"

He grinds his cock into my ass and holy hell, he's hard as a rock. When I don't answer right away, he smacks my bottom again.

"I don't have a condom in here with me, baby. I'm clean and haven't been with anyone in almost a year."

"I'm clean too and I'm on birth control. I haven't been with anyone for almost two years," I whimper.

He grunts. "Are you okay with me fucking you bare?"

A moan escapes as he presses his hardness along my slit. "Yes."

As soon as the word is out, he slams into my pussy, making me scream. He grips my hips so hard I think they'll bruise but it feels so good and when he pulls almost completely out and slams into me again, I almost come right then and there.

"You're going to learn there isn't a single fucking thing in this world I wouldn't do to make sure you're taken care of."

His words hit me deep in my chest as he starts fucking me harder. He fills me completely and the crown of his cock massages that delicate spot inside just perfectly.

"Who do you belong to, baby?" he growls in my ear.

"Oh, God!"

He chuckles. "No, baby. Not him. You belong to me. You're mine and this pretty little pussy I'm fucking right now is mine. So goddamn perfect, just like you."

My entire body tenses at his declaration, and my orgasm explodes. At the same time, he starts fucking me erratically as he chases his own release. We both cry out as we ride the waves of the rollercoaster until we nearly collapse.

He lifts me in his arms and steps out of the shower before he sets me down, grabs a towel, and wraps it around me. I feel like a limp noodle and have to keep one hand on his chest for balance as he dons his own towel, then grabs a third and starts drying me off from head to toe.

I'm in a daze, high from my orgasms but also thinking about everything he said while he was fucking me. Did he mean it? If he didn't mean it, I'll be crushed and humiliated. So, I spend the next several hours unable to concentrate on the movies we're watching. No, my mind is back in the shower, wondering if I might mean something to Jaxon Sawyer or if he says those kinds of things to every woman he has sex with. At least my cramps have subsided almost completely thanks to the delicious orgasms and care he's given me.

20

JAXON

My girl is panicking inside. I see it in her eyes. She's sitting stiffly against me while we watch movies. If I'm totally honest, I'm panicking too. I meant the things I said while we were in the shower. She's mine. At least, I want her to be mine. I want to belong to her too.

At the same time, I want to run for my life. This woman could destroy me, and I've already gone through enough dark times. I wouldn't survive more. She doesn't want a relationship. She's made that clear. I need to respect that and go back to my house. We need to go back to being neighbors. My feelings for her will go away eventually, but not unless I keep her at a distance. There's really no reason for me to see her other than as a neighbor.

We watch three movies and, when it starts getting late, I feed her a can of chicken noodle soup because she said that sounded good. Afterward, I get her in bed, set up the heating pad under her back, and give her another dose of medicine. Then I kiss her forehead. Both of us have been quiet since the shower. It's obvious we're in our own heads wondering what to do.

"If you need anything tomorrow, text me, okay? I can bring you anything you need. Call day or night. I'm right next door."

She's clutching Buttercup to her chest as she smiles sweetly. "Thank you, Jaxon. I really appreciate you coming over here. I'm sorry that I wasn't a very good patient, but you really did make me feel better."

I smile, ignoring the tightness in my chest. She called me by my name, not Daddy. I kiss her forehead again. "You were a perfectly fine patient. I'm just glad that you're feeling better. That's all that matters. I'll lock up on my way out."

I grab her pacifier and slide it between her lips, then let myself out of her house with my dog trailing behind me.

The air is cold and crisp, and the November fog is settling in. I stand outside for a few minutes to feel it, hoping it will help me think more clearly. I've never been so confused in my life. I want her, but I don't want to want her. I need to talk to one of my friends. It's only eight, so maybe Silas will meet me at the bar for a beer. I shoot off a text and he replies immediately, saying that he'll meet me at The Tap Room in ten minutes. I put Willie in the house and grab my truck keys and a jacket.

He's already sitting at the bar when I get there with three ice cold beers set in front of him.

"Dane's on his way too. So, what's wrong?" he asks when I sit down.

I give him a sideways glance. "What makes you think there's something wrong?"

He shrugs. "Well, it's eight o'clock on a work night and you wanted to meet for a beer. So, something had to have happened between you and your cutie pie neighbor."

I let out a low growl and glare at him. He shoots me a smug grin. I don't like him calling her a cutie pie. The only one who should call her that is me.

"Yeah, well, something did happen, and I don't really

know what to think about it. My head's a mess right now. I don't know how to handle it."

Silas takes a drink of his beer at the same time Dane sits down.

"What's going on?" he asks.

Silas tips his beer toward me. "Jaxon's fucking things up with Leah."

I glare at my best friend and flip him the bird. "What the fuck? I never said anything about messing it up. I'm just confused. I like this girl, but you know me, I don't want a relationship. We were just supposed to have a one-night thing but she wasn't feeling well today, and I went to take care of her because I wanted to. Because I couldn't stand the thought of her being there alone to fend for herself. And honestly, I loved taking care of her. I didn't want to leave. But we're just friends. She doesn't want a relationship either."

Both men stare at me for a long time.

"What?" I demand.

"Did she tell you that? About not wanting a relationship?" Silas asks.

"Yes. She was very clear about it and so was I."

Dane shakes his head. "I've never seen a woman look at you the way she does and I've never seen you look at a woman the way you look at her. You never looked at Wendy like that."

Just my ex's name being brought up makes me tense. "Yeah, well, shit with me and Wendy was different. It was hard to look at her like that. She was never happy with me because I was never able to do anything right. I could never give her what she needed. I was a failure to her."

Silas scoffs and shakes his head. "You're a damn idiot."

I turn to my best friend. "Why am I an idiot? What did I do?"

Dane snorts. "Nothing anybody does for Wendy is good

enough. It never has been. And you're selling yourself short. You bent over backwards for that woman. You worked your ass off for her. You gave her everything she wanted and needed. And she was still unhappy. It wasn't you that fucked up. It was her. And you need to get that through your thick skull. She screwed you over just like she did to her second and third husbands. Most women aren't like that. Leah isn't like that. You can look into her eyes and see how pure and sweet she is. There's no hidden agenda for her. That woman loves you."

I swallow my sip of beer. "No, she doesn't love me. We've only known each other for a few weeks."

Silas shrugs. "There is such a thing as love at first sight, you know."

I shake my head. "She was dressed in a bear costume the first time I saw her. I'm pretty sure I didn't fall in love at first sight."

My friends both laugh. Thinking about her in that cute little bear onesie makes me smile. So sweet, so innocent down on her knees, petting my dog like he was her longtime best friend. Maybe it was love at first sight. It doesn't matter, though. I can't risk getting hurt.

Dane gives Silas a look, and Silas shrugs. "Yeah, I know, dude. He's going to do it the hard way. He's going to torture himself, and eventually he'll come around. Just hope she doesn't find another Daddy before that happens."

Anger rushes through my veins at the idea of any other man even looking at her. Sometimes I don't know why I'm friends with these assholes. They always talk shit and know exactly what to say to get under my skin.

"Silas, are you seriously going to tell me that after your divorce you weren't damaged? That you're not still damaged?" I ask.

Silas shrugs. "I'm not going to say it didn't hurt. Of course it did. I was with her for years, but we weren't meant to be together. Granted, she didn't do the shit to me that Wendy did, so I can't say my ego was hurt like yours was. But one thing I do know is that spending the rest of your life alone is no way to live."

I groan because he's not totally wrong. I love my dog. He's good company. He doesn't talk back. He eats whatever I feed him. He's low maintenance. But I'm still lonely. Daddying Leah has awoken something in me that has been asleep for so long, I didn't even realize how much I missed it.

Silas takes a drink of his beer and sets it down on the bar. "On a change of subject. Did you guys hear Summer Pierce is moving back to town?"

Dane tenses beside me.

I shrug. "I hadn't heard. I just know her mom hasn't been doing well, so maybe she's moving back to take care of her."

Silas sighs. "Yeah, that's probably it. The poor girl's had a rough life. I'm surprised she wants to come back here at all after the way some of the people treated her family."

Dane shrugs, suddenly looking irritated. "Whatever it is, I'm sure that she won't be here for long. Greer will be happy to see her, though."

"Dude, are you ever going to tell us what happened between you and her?" I ask.

My friend shakes his head. "Nothing happened between us. She's Greer's best friend, that's all."

I don't believe my friend for one second. First of all, he's a terrible liar and second of all, any time her name is brought up, he always gets tense.

Around ten, we decide to call it a night.

"Thanks for listening to me. I appreciate it," I say as we make our way to the parking lot.

Silas slaps me on the back. "You never know what could happen. You just need to give it a chance. If you don't, you'll constantly be asking yourself, what if? I can tell you this: that woman cares for you, and she's not the type of woman to walk away from. Any man would be lucky to call her his."

I tip my head up to the starry sky. "I know. I just don't know if I have it in me to try another relationship."

I give Dane a back-slapping hug. "Thanks for coming out."

He returns the affection and grins. "I agree with Silas. I think Leah would be a very good woman and Little girl for you. Greer had wonderful things to say about her and it sounded like Leah had some good things to say about you when the girls hung out. Which is surprising because you're boring as hell."

I laugh and flip both my friends off before getting into my truck and heading home. I feel better after talking to them, but I still don't know what to do about the woman that lives next door.

All her lights are still off when I pull into my driveway, and I want to go over there and check on her to make sure she's still feeling okay. I want to crawl into bed with her and wrap my body around hers. But I don't. Instead, I go into my lonely house and get into bed with one-eyed Willie who's thrilled to sleep in his human's bed.

LEAH IS ALREADY GONE by the time I leave my house the next morning. She goes to work early to get delivery orders ready, but I would have liked to have seen her in person so I could make sure she's okay. I should have woken up earlier. While my truck warms up, I send her a text.

> Jaxon: Hey, Little bear, how are you feeling?

When she doesn't respond right away, I leave for work. Maybe I'll stop by Blossom and Bloom later and check on her. My hope is that she's feeling better. I hated seeing her in so much pain.

My conversation with Dane and Silas last night is still running through my mind. I definitely wasn't faultless in my marriage to Wendy, but I did stay faithful and loyal. I wasn't perfect by any means. No one is. She always said I stifled her, but I never stopped her from going out with friends or going on girls' trips or doing the things that she wanted to do so I think really it was that being married to me stifled the life she wanted to lead. Having to be accountable to someone and follow the rules we had both agreed on for our dynamic. She made the choice to get into someone else's bed instead of talking to me so we could figure out how to adjust. That was on her.

I hate to admit it—and I'll never say it out loud to the guys—but they were right. Fuck, I hate when they're right. I don't want Leah as my neighbor, and I don't want to be her friend. I want to be her Daddy and her man. I want to check on her and constantly make sure she's not doing dangerous shit that's going to get her hurt. I want to cuddle her, bathe her, put her to bed at night and wake up with her in the mornings. I think that might be what she wants too. I've been wrong before, though, so who knows? Until we have a conversation, I don't know where we stand.

The thing is, to have that conversation, I need to grow a set of balls and actually go to her. I'm going to wait until she's doing better, though. She told me when she's on her period, she's extra emotional and I don't want to do anything that's going to cause her additional stress. We both need to be clear headed when we have the conversation. And if she decides that she doesn't want to move forward with me, I'll have to respect that. We both told each other exactly what we wanted when we first hooked up. I should have known that one hookup wasn't going to be enough. Hell, I should have known when I met her in that damn bear onesie that I would never get enough of Leah Day.

Silas doesn't pester me about what we talked about last night. Instead, we work on Asher's renovation. He's updating the kitchen. The old house he bought a few blocks away from mine is in desperate need of work. It's definitely a holdout from the seventies. I'm thankful for the silence of the day as we work. Something about using my hands while getting sweaty and dirty helps me think clearly.

I'm tired, though. As much as I love my dog, he definitely isn't as good of a cuddle partner as Leah. He snores like a damn freight train. Who knew a dog could snore so loud? Jesus, how had I not heard him before? And of course, because I couldn't sleep, I worried about my girl all night long.

I still have so many questions about what will happen if we decide to start a relationship? Will we move in together? Will she move in with me? Will she want me to move into that horrible house of hers? I'd do it if she wanted me to. Hell, I'd do just about anything for her. All she has to do is look at me with those pouty lips and sweet blue eyes and I'm putty in her hands. Doesn't mean I won't paddle her ass if she's naughty, but I'll still pretty much give her whatever she wants as long as she's being safe.

I'm getting way ahead of myself. We've only known each other for a few weeks. We're not going to move in together tomorrow. We're not getting married tomorrow. Although the thought of marching her down to the courthouse and changing her last name to mine has an appeal to it. I'm really fucked in the head right now. This woman has me all tied up in knots and I am going to get so much shit from my friends about this.

Most of us have been avoiding serious relationships for some time. We're all at an age where we've been burned in one way or another and we're bitter. My girl makes me not want to be bitter anymore. She's the sunshine to my darkness.

When Asher gets home from work, Silas and I call it a day.

"You guys want a beer?" Asher offers.

We grunt our acceptance, and the three of us sit back to have a drink together.

"So, are you ready to stop being a pussy and avoiding how you really feel about Leah?" Silas asks.

God, he's an asshole. I can't wait until he meets a woman he's hung up on. I'm going to give him so much shit.

Asher grins. "My guess is no, but Jaxon isn't a total idiot. He's got to see how special she is. Hell, I'd get my act together for her."

I stare at both of them with a murderous scowl. "She hasn't been feeling well the past couple of days, so I'm going to wait until she's better. I do want more. I want to be her Daddy and her man. There's no way I can just be casual with Leah. I care about her. Fuck, I more than care about her."

Both my friends grin at me and hold their bottles up. We clink our beers, but soon we call it a night and go our separate ways. Leah texted me back earlier in the day, saying she was feeling better and that she was still having some cramps, but not nearly as bad as before. I wish she would have stayed home another day, but I also understand that she feels like she has to go to work since she's new to her job.

I get home, let Willie out, take a shower, do all the things I need to do before I go over there to check on her in person. On the off chance that I end up staying the night, I don't want to crawl into bed with a bunch of sawdust all over me and get her all dirty. She's too precious for that.

The sun is just starting to go down. This time of year is depressing. It gets dark way too early and gets light way too late. At least it's a good excuse to cuddle. I leave Willie at home for now. I'll come back and get him if I end up staying the night. Just as I'm walking off my porch, a fancy BMW pulls into Leah's driveway. A man gets out with a bouquet of red roses in his hand. What the fuck?

He walks up to the door and knocks. Is she going out on a date with this dipshit? He looks like a slimy tool.

Who is he? He's definitely not from Pine Hollow. Because of dusk settling, I can't see her face when she opens the door, and I can't hear what they say to each other over the wind. After a brief second, the man walks inside and the door closes.

My chest feels like it's caving in. I'm not stupid enough to think that red roses mean nothing. But obviously I'm stupid enough to think I might mean something to Leah. I should have known better. I always come second and I'm an idiot for wanting more. How could I have let my feelings get involved?

I think this hurts worse than when I found out Wendy was sleeping around, but I'm not going to compete with another man. If I'm not her first and only choice, I don't want to be part of her life. It sucks but I'll get over her. I'll just be pissed off and bitter about it for a while before that happens.

21

LEAH

I expected Jaxon to be at my doorstep when I opened the door. But he's not. It's my ex-husband.

"What are you doing here?" I snap.

He's holding roses. Of all the flowers in the world, roses are my least favorite. I don't like them because they're so common. If someone wants to impress me with flowers, I want something rarer like Ocean Breeze Orchids. The most annoying thing is he knows I hate roses. He doesn't give a shit, though.

"Hey, baby."

I cringe at him calling me baby. It makes me want to vomit.

"Kevin, what are you doing here?"

He steps inside without an invitation and closes the door. What the hell? How does he even know where I live? I purposely didn't give him my forwarding address and our divorce was final before I moved here so my new address wasn't on any of our legal documents.

"You don't look happy to see me."

I can't stop myself from rolling my eyes. "We're divorced. Why would I be happy to see you? We're not together anymore, Kevin. Why are you at my house? And how did you even get my address?"

He pulls an envelope from his pocket. "This came in the mail for you."

When I snatch it from his hand, I realize it's open. I look at it. It's a verification letter from my bank confirming that my mailing address was successfully changed to my current address. What the hell? The bank will be getting a call from me tomorrow.

I press my lips together, trying to keep myself under control. "Why did you open my mail?"

"I didn't know if it was something important."

I blink rapidly several times in total disbelief because whether it was important or not, he shouldn't have opened it.

"Here, I brought you these." He tries to hand me the roses, but I don't take them.

"I don't like roses and you know that. Again, what are you doing here?"

I'm in total disbelief. My period is making me cranky and seeing this man's face is making me even crankier. He's the last person on earth that I want to see.

"I missed you and I wanted to see you," he says before running his tongue over the front of his teeth.

He always runs his tongue over his teeth when he's lying. I should have caught onto that a long time ago and maybe I would have realized he'd been cheating on me a lot sooner than I did.

"Well, I don't miss you, Kevin. We divorced for a reason. I moved away from Portland for a reason."

He looks around my house. "And I see you downgraded. This place is, uh, something."

My hackles rise as he insults my new house. "This house may not be as new and nice as the house we lived in, but it's more of a home to me than ours ever was."

He rubs his chest like I hurt him. "Ouch. You certainly have your claws out today, don't you?"

"Kevin, you need to leave. I don't want you here, and I don't want to see you."

He straightens his shoulders and puffs up his chest. "Oh, come on. Thanksgiving is coming up. Let's spend the holiday together, we can go over to my parents."

I'm seriously about to lose my mind with this man. He doesn't belong here. The only person I want here is Jaxon. "Over my dead body would I go to your parents' house for Thanksgiving. They hate me."

He runs his tongue over his teeth. "They don't hate you, they adore you. They think you're great. They don't know that we got divorced, so just come to Thanksgiving. They'll be thrilled to see you."

I scrub a hand over my face, completely baffled right now. Am I getting punked? "What do you mean they don't know we're divorced?"

"Well, you know how they are. They're old fashioned and they don't believe in divorce."

Oh my God. He has to leave, like, right now. I don't want to see his face. I want nothing to do with him. And I am *pissed* that he opened my mail to find out where I lived.

"Your family hates me. There's no fucking way I'm going to Thanksgiving."

Kevin gives me that look, the one I've always hated. It's the one that tells me he completely disapproves of what I just said. "That's not any language to use. Come on. Just come."

I throw my hand on my hip. "Why are you so insistent that I come to Thanksgiving with your parents? They *hate* me. I don't like them, and I don't like *you*."

He glares at me. "You might not like me, but we were married for several years so you owe me this."

My mouth drops open. "I was married to you for several

years while you were fucking who knows how many women."

I can see the anger in his dark brown eyes. It's the look he would get before he would insult me. Suddenly, like a switch is flipped, his anger disappears. He flashes me his perfectly white smile. That's what he does best. Turns on that fake charm and manipulates people to get what he wants. That's what he did to me. I was so young when we met. My parents had just died, and I was sad and lonely. He seemed like this wonderful guy, and he manipulated me into thinking I was safe to be myself with him. How blind could I have been?

"I know you're not a fan of my parents. But you know, my father is very strict about not making me partner in the firm unless I'm married. He's been putting it off and he finally told my mom he was ready to do it, and he's going to announce it at Thanksgiving. If I show up divorced, there's no way he's going to make me partner."

I seriously cannot believe my ears right now. That he thinks I would do one single thing for him after everything that he put me through. The insults. The cheating. Fighting with me in court over every single asset. I was lucky that I even got part of the proceeds from the sale of our house. The only reason I did is because I had used all of my parents' life insurance to help buy that house. He'd insisted it was the perfect home for us and we'd be happy there. I'm not doing another thing for this man.

I march around him and swing the front door open. "Get out of my house. We're done. Don't ever talk to me. Don't ever call me. Don't ever show up here again. If you do, I'll file for a restraining order."

He runs his tongue over his teeth, and I contemplate punching him and knocking them all out.

"Come on, Leah. You know I love you."

That statement makes me burst out laughing. I'm

Jaxon

laughing so hard that I'm cackling. I sound like the Wicked Witch of the East in complete hysteria.

"You don't love me. You've never loved me. You loved that I was vulnerable, and you knew I would give you whatever you wanted in return for your affection. I'm not that girl anymore. You took everything away from me. My friends, my freedom, my happiness, my self-esteem. You beat me down with your words and mind games every day for years, all while you were out fucking other women. It's not happening, Kevin. I'm not going to Thanksgiving dinner with you. You can tell your family to fuck right off, and you can fuck right off, too."

He storms past me, shoving the flowers against my chest. "You know the least you could do is be a decent woman and do me this one last favor. Once I make partner, you can have nothing to do with me."

I take hold of the flowers and chuck them into the front yard. "You can take your ugly red roses and go fuck yourself. Because there's no way I'm doing a damn thing with you. I pretended enough over the years. I pretended to orgasm, I pretended to be happy, I pretended everything was okay, but it was all a lie. So, leave now, before I call the police."

Kevin stares at me for a long moment. "You always were just a fat bitch with an attitude. You didn't know your place. If you would have, you'd be able to live a cushy lifestyle. But no. Now you want to live in this run-down shitty house in this shitty little town. Well, that's fine. You live that way. I'll be living the good life, especially now that I don't have to deal with you."

This time my laugh is genuine. "This town has welcomed me and made me feel like I finally have a place to call home. Even though I don't have family anymore, the people here are my family. So you can disrespect my house, you can say as much negative bullshit about me as you want, but I don't care because it's not true. I love this house. I love this town.

And for the first time in a long time, I'm finally starting to love myself. I don't love you, though. Now get off my lawn and take those cheap flowers with you!"

Damn. That felt good.

Kevin huffs as he stomps off to his BMW. "You're coming to Thanksgiving, Leah. We'll have fun. It will be like old times."

Before my head actually explodes, he gets into his car and drives away. Suddenly, I'm exhausted. Just seeing him took every ounce of energy I had and sucked it all out. All I want to do is go knock on Jaxon's door, crawl into his lap and snuggle up in the safety of his arms. I haven't heard from him since this morning, though, and I don't want to be clingy.

He took care of me yesterday. But we're not together. I can't just show up on his doorstep expecting him to hold me. I care for him more than I'd like to admit. I'm sure we'll see each other this week in our driveways, or he'll send me a text to check on me, because that's just how Jaxon is.

So instead of doing what I want to do, I trudge back inside and drop onto the couch. Nothing like a fight with your asshole ex to become completely mentally drained. It doesn't take long before I fall asleep right where I am because I don't have the energy tonight to go to my room.

THE REST of the week goes by in a blur. I haven't heard from Jaxon since Wednesday morning. I miss him immensely. I even texted him on Thursday afternoon and asked if he'd had a good day. He never responded. That hurt more than I'd like to admit.

So, when Natalie, Bree, and Greer texted about going out to The Tap Room tonight, I begrudgingly agreed. Moping around my house will get nothing accomplished. I

Jaxon

have to get it into my head that Jaxon and I are only neighbors. He didn't want anything more from me than the one night even if his actions said otherwise. If only my heart would remember that.

I choose a ruby red knitted baby doll dress to wear. It's long sleeve and just because I'm feeling grumpy, I purposely don't grab a jacket. I'm wearing the same shoes I wore the night Jaxon and I had sex. After adding just a dab of makeup and spending a few minutes curling the ends of my hair, I head out to meet my friends.

A night of drinks sounds good. Maybe it'll get my mind off my hot neighbor. Bree, Natalie and Greer are in the parking lot waiting for me when I arrive. I feel so lucky to be part of their friend group.

"Hey, you look so cute," Bree practically shouts from across the parking lot.

I plaster on the best smile I can and give them all a hug. "Oh my gosh, I've missed you guys."

We make our way into the bar, and it's already packed. It seems like this is the place to be on Saturday nights. As soon as we walk in, the hair on the back of my neck rises. I look around and every nerve in my body freezes as my eyes land on Jaxon, whose arm is around a beautiful woman. I watch as he presses a kiss to the side of her head and laughs at whatever she just said.

My body temperature rises, and I grind my teeth together. We might have only agreed on one night, but the time we spent together was much more than that whether he wants to admit it or not. Now he's suddenly cuddled up with some other woman less than a week after I was calling him Daddy and he was fucking me bare?

I actually thought maybe he cared about me but was fighting it. My chest aches. But my anger flares.

"Oh, fuck no," is all I say before I start stomping toward them.

"Leah, wait! You don't understand!" Greer calls out.

I ignore her and make my way across the bar to where Jaxon is hanging out with his friends and this woman who now has her arms wrapped around his waist and is hugging him.

With my index finger, I jab him in the shoulder. "Hey."

He turns and looks down at me, his expression unreadable.

"Seriously? You were just at my house the other day, taking care of me, being intimate with me, and now you're here with another woman."

Something flashes across his face I can't decipher. A mix of surprise and anger maybe? Well, he shouldn't be surprised. This is a small town and we're in the only bar. Of course he would run into me at some point.

Then to my complete surprise, the woman smiles broadly at me. "You must be Leah. Oh my gosh, I've heard all about you. I'm Sara. I'm Jaxon's sister!"

All the blood drains from my face as Jaxon hits me with a smug grin. "Yeah, this is my sister, Sara. Sara, this is Leah, my *neighbor*."

The way he emphasizes the word neighbor stings and it also pisses me off. Is that all I was to him when he was fucking me? When his face was between my thighs? Just his neighbor?

Narrowing my eyes at him, I shake my head, spin on my heel, and stomp out of the bar. My friends gape at me as I storm past them. I'm pissed. I just humiliated myself in front of the man I'm in love with and the entire freaking town of Pine Hollow watched. And yes. Love. I'm in love with Jaxon.

I'm glad it's dark out so people in the parking lot can't see the tears streaming down my face. How did I get this wrapped up in a man when I swore to myself I wasn't going to get involved in another relationship?

"Little girl!" Jaxon calls out.

He comes storming up behind me. "What do you think you're doing?"

"I'm leaving. I'm going home to lick my wounds and die of embarrassment."

He glares at me and shakes his head. "I don't even know why you're jealous in the first place. You're the one who had a man at your house the other day bringing you flowers."

My mouth drops open and the anger I felt just a few minutes ago returns. "Are you kidding me? That was my ex-husband who came to my house trying to manipulate me into going to Thanksgiving with his parents so he can make partner at his father's law firm. And you know what, Jaxon? If you had checked on me and asked about it, or responded to my text message, you would know that I threw him out of my house and told him never to speak to me again."

This time the blood drains out of his face as I swipe my tears with the back of my hands.

I raise my eyebrows at him, my hands on my hips as I start pacing. "You know, I thought I could do this casual thing. I thought we could just fuck and get it out of our systems, and that would be it. I thought that would be enough, but it's not, Jaxon. You have shown me a side of you that I didn't think existed when I first met you. In the time that we've spent together, all the small things that you've done, all the sweet things you've said, it's all added up and I've fallen for you, and I don't know how to handle it because I don't want to just be your neighbor and I don't want to just be your friend."

"Okay," he says.

I stop mid step and look at him.

"What do you mean 'okay'? You have nothing to say to all of that, but okay?" I demand as I stomp my foot.

Yes, I'm acting like a brat and having a slight tantrum right now, but I don't care.

"Oh, I have a lot to say to that," he growls as he stomps toward me. "The first thing I'm going to say is that I care about you, Little girl. I've cared about you since the day I met you, and I don't want to just be your neighbor or your friend. I want to be your Daddy and your man. I want to be your confidant. Your rock. Your protector. And I want to be the man you come to when you're not feeling well, or when you have a bad dream, or when you need to be cuddled. I want you to be my Little girl. And not just casually. I can't do casual with you. I don't know why I thought I could, but I can't. You may have fallen for me, but I fell for you too."

Suddenly, I can't breathe. I'm frozen replaying his words. Before I can ask any questions, he grabs my hair and crushes his mouth to mine, kissing me possessively, his other hand pulling me against his erection.

When he finally releases my mouth, I'm panting. "You're up to three spankings. We're going to handle those tonight before bed, and then we're going to sit down and talk about your rules, our dynamic, and our relationship. Then we're going to decide where we go from here. But I can tell you one thing, Little girl. You. Are. Mine. And there is no one else in this world for me. I will never, ever cheat on you or entertain any other woman's attention."

Tears roll down my cheeks. "I would never cheat on you either, Jaxon. I'm not that kind of person, and I know that kind of pain. I would never do that to you. I care for you too much."

He uses the pads of his thumbs to wipe my tears. "I hate seeing you cry. I never want to be the one to cause you to be sad."

I sniffle and lean into his touch, loving the security of it. When he wraps his arms around me again, I melt. We stand in the cold parking lot for several minutes hugging each other, the sound of country music floating through the air.

When he pulls back, he presses a kiss to both of my

cheeks, then my forehead, then my lips. They're soft and sweet, and they cause butterflies to flutter in my tummy.

"Now let's go inside and enjoy the evening together. I want you to actually meet my sister. I told her all about you and she's so excited to get to know you."

I glance toward the entrance of the bar. "I'm pretty sure that I don't ever want to step foot in there again. All your friends, your sister, and now my friends probably think I've lost my mind. I need to move out of Pine Hollow."

He chuckles. "Oh, baby girl, you're not moving anywhere, and nobody thinks you've lost your mind. We've all had our moments. And believe me, you're not the first person to cause a scene in the middle of the bar. Remind me to tell you the story about Summer Pierce throwing a beer at Dane years ago. Or the time Belle Miller broke up a bar fight between two huge dudes and hit both of them in the head with a tray. Or when Austin punched some guy for grabbing Greer's ass."

My eyes widen. I have no idea who these Summer or Belle women are, but I think I already like them.

"Now if I have to put you over my shoulder and carry you in there myself, I will. But I'd rather you walk in with me hand in hand."

I slide my arms around his waist and rest my face against his chest, listening to his heartbeat. "I've missed you the past few days. I was so sad you didn't respond to my text."

He strokes my back. "I'm sorry. That was my fault. I should have talked to you. I've been hurt too, baby. Sometimes my mind plays tricks on me, and I think the worst. You and I need to agree that if we're ever feeling insecure, we need to talk to each other about it. That way we can clarify any misconceptions we might have. Is that a deal?"

"Yeah, that's a deal."

"Come on. I bet you haven't eaten dinner yet, have you?"

I look up at him with a sheepish smile. "I hate that you know me so well."

He tugs me by the hand. "I don't. It just means I get to take care of you."

We make our way toward the entrance, but I stop halfway there. "Wait, why am I up to three spankings?"

He lets out a low growl. "Because it's thirty degrees out and you don't have a goddamn coat."

Crap. I should have known that would come back to haunt me. I have a feeling I won't be sitting very comfortably for the rest of the weekend.

22

JAXON

I keep my arm wrapped protectively around Leah as we make our way back into the bar. Her friends joined my sister and my friends, and when we reach them, they smile and act like nothing happened.

Sara pulls Leah into a hug. "I knew my brother would pull his head out of his ass. We totally need to hang out. Oh, and I hope you'll join us for Thanksgiving. My parents wanted to make sure you know you're welcome and we'd love to have you."

Leah looks up at me with wide, questioning eyes. My sister can be a bit much sometimes but in the best way possible. There's no doubt in my mind my family will love my girl. What's not to love? She's amazing and even though my sister is a total brat most of the time, she's right about me pulling my head out of my ass. Not that I'll ever admit it.

We wave over Belle, one of the bartenders.

"Hey, you guys. What are you having?" Belle asks.

After we order our drinks, I introduce Leah. Belle grins and immediately gives my girl a hug.

"I've heard about you! It's so nice to finally meet you. Everyone's had nothing but good things to say. We'll have to hang out sometime. Greer, send me Leah's number and give her mine."

Again, Leah looks up at me with wide questioning eyes. I lower my face to hers. "See, you're not going anywhere. This is your home now and this town is your family."

She leans into me and sighs. "Yeah. I think you're right about that."

We spend the rest of the evening drinking, eating, and telling stories. After three drinks, I cut Leah off. I want her to be sober by the time we get home. We're going to have a conversation and she's going to experience her very first punishment. I've put both of those things off long enough.

Around eleven, I tell her to say her goodbyes. She doesn't argue with me. Having friends is important to her, as it should be, and I'll never get in the way of her hanging out with them or having a girls' night but tonight, I need to get her home.

I walk her to her front door, wait until she's inside, and go get Willie from my house. He's thrilled to see her, and she seems just as excited to see him as she drops to her knees to give him some belly rubs. I shouldn't feel jealous of my dog but I do.

After a few minutes, I tell Willie to go lie down then lead Leah over to the couch.

"I'm going to make a snack and get you some water. I want you to start thinking about your hard limits because we're going to go over them tonight."

Her breathing quickens but she nods, and I leave her to make a plate of cheese and crackers for us. When I return, Leah sits with her legs curled under her and she chews nervously on her bottom lip.

Once I set the plate down, I sit and pat my lap. "Come here, Little bear."

I'm pleased when she immediately crawls over to me and climbs into my arms.

"Why do you look so nervous? Are you having second thoughts?"

I hate feeling so insecure but after what I went through with Wendy, I still have parts of me that are damaged and scared.

Leah's eyes widen, and she shakes her head. "What? No. Not at all. I'm scared, Jaxon. It would truly break me if you hurt me."

I quietly chuckle. "You know, I'm scared too, baby girl. How about we be scared together and show each other what it's like to truly be cared for by another person?"

Her eyes fill with tears but she's smiling. "I'd really like that."

We sit in silence for a few minutes, and I start feeding her crackers and cheese. When we finish, I set the plate to the side and pull her against my chest.

"Tell Daddy why being tied up is a hard limit for you."

She stiffens. I hate that, but I don't say anything. Instead, I wait for her to gather her thoughts and answer.

"Kevin tied me up once. He made the restraints so tight my hands were turning blue and when I asked him to untie me, he wouldn't. It had been my idea to try restraints, so he insisted I didn't really want to be untied. It was hours before he finally released me. I didn't have feeling in my hands for several days after that, so I went to the doctor. They did some tests and I had nerve damage."

"Mother fucking bastard," I growl, my hands gripping her hips.

She jolts back and the pain in her eyes kills a piece of me inside.

"I'm going to murder him. I'm going to hunt him down and fucking bury the bastard."

"He's not worth it, Jaxon. Besides, his father is a ruthless lawyer, and I don't want him to put you in jail for the rest of your life for killing his son."

I shake my head, barely able to contain the rage burning inside me. Bastards like her ex have no business living in this world.

"Anyway, that's why it's a limit. It didn't scare me when you used your hands to restrain me, but I don't think I ever want you to use actual restraints."

"Was the physical damage permanent?" I already know the emotional part is permanent and I'm going to spend the rest of my life trying to undo the pain he caused.

"Luckily, no. The doctor put both my wrists in braces, so I wasn't able to work for several weeks but they healed without surgery."

"I'll never use restraints on you, but I need you to understand that this is why I insist on a safeword. I will always respect that word. In this kind of dynamic, there will be times when you tell me to stop but I know that doesn't always mean stop. Using your safeword, though, will bring everything to a halt immediately. Do you understand me?"

She bobs her head. "Yes. I trust you, Jaxon. I trust you more than I ever trusted him, and it was stupid of me to suggest restraints."

I want to shake her a little because no, it wasn't stupid of her. The only person to blame is her ex.

"That's four," I growl.

Her eyes widen. "What?"

"That's four punishments. I don't ever want to hear you refer to yourself as stupid. The only person at fault here is him. Got it?"

The dramatic sigh she lets out almost makes me smile.

"You're kind of stubborn," she murmurs.

That makes me smile. "Yes. I am. I'm very stubborn. But, I will always respect your limits and boundaries and I will always honor your safeword."

She snuggles into my chest. "I know."

Jaxon

Those two little words mean the world to me. "What are your other hard limits?"

"I don't really know. I mean, I'm not into knife play or blood play or anything like that. Although, having sex while I was on my period wasn't terrible."

I chuckle. "That wasn't blood play, baby. So sex on your period isn't a hard limit?"

She thinks for a moment. "I don't think so but could we do it in the shower like before? I really don't want to clean up a homicide scene after we get busy."

Oh my God. This Little girl makes me laugh more than I've ever laughed in my life. "Deal. No homicide scenes. What else?"

"I think that's it. I haven't tried a ton of stuff so I might figure out something later that I won't want to try. Is that okay?"

With my thumb and index finger, I pinch her chin and force her to look up at me. "You can always change any limits. It doesn't matter if it was never a limit before, you can make it one at any time. Communication is the most important thing in this dynamic. I can't read your mind, so I need you to always talk to me, okay?"

Her gaze softens and her eyes fill with tears. "I think I'm in love with you, Jaxon Sawyer."

The backs of my eyes burn, and I have to swallow several times before I can reply. "I know I'm in love with you, Leah Day."

We kiss and hold each other for a long time. My girl surprises me when she pulls away and looks at me nervously.

"Can we get my punishments over with? I've been anxious about them all night and my tummy is fluttery with nerves."

"Yes. We can. Thank you for telling me that. I don't ever want to cause you excess anxiety. Normally I would deal with a punishment at the time the crime is committed but I won't if you're not feeling well, which is why you have four built up."

She groans, and I chuckle. "Don't worry, Little bear. Since this is your first one, I'll go easy on you and only use my hand. In the future, you'll meet other implements, though. Got it?"

Her pupils dilate and she squirms on my lap, making my cock ache. It's going to kill me not to fuck her tonight, but I'll just have to suffer. I won't reward her with orgasms after a punishment. If only she knew it was punishment for me too.

When she finally nods, I ask, "Are you still on your period?"

"No. This one only lasted a couple of days. Sometimes they last for weeks and sometimes they're really short."

"Okay. Let's go to your room, baby."

23

LEAH

My ass is sweating I'm so nervous. Tonight has been a whirlwind. In the best way possible. But now, it's time to pay the piper. I trust him. More than I've ever trusted anyone. I know Jaxon won't harm me. But his hands are huge, and I have a feeling his idea of "taking it easy on me" might not be the same as mine.

He takes my hand and leads me into the bedroom. I'm relieved when he only turns on the bedside lamp. I'm not sure what to expect or what I'm supposed to do, so I twist my fingers together nervously. To my surprise, he comes to me and slides his hand into my hair at the nape of my neck, then kisses me. It's possessive yet intimate, and I melt.

When he pulls his lips from mine, he stares down at me. "I know you're nervous. We're in this together, okay? If it gets to be too much or too painful, what are you supposed to do?"

I swallow. "Say red."

"That's my good girl. Come here."

He sits on the edge of my bed and positions me between his thighs, resting his big hands on my hips. "First rule in this dynamic? No lying. You told me you were fine the other day when you were clearly in pain. I can't take care of you properly if you're not honest with me."

"I'm sorry," I whisper.

"I know. I'm going to make sure you're very sorry by the time we're done. Second rule, no talking badly about yourself. You're perfect. Smart, caring, kind, sassy, funny, beautiful, sexy. I don't ever want to hear you put yourself down because I'm not going to allow anyone to hurt my girl, including you. Understand?"

"Yes, Daddy." My voice is quiet and unsure. I can't stop fidgeting but despite my nerves, there's a calm inside me. He's not yelling at me or calling me names. He's not bullying me or ignoring me. He's patiently explaining why I've earned my punishment and he's setting rules that are fair and thought out.

His eyes sparkle. "I love hearing you call me Daddy. I want you to call me that from now on."

I return his smile, my cheeks on fire. "Okay, Daddy. I like it too."

"Rule number three, if the temperature is below fifty degrees, you wear a jacket. The last thing I need is you catching a cold or getting frostbite."

That makes me giggle. "Colds are caused by viruses, not the actual cold, Daddy."

The corner of his eye twitches, and I remember the predicament I'm in. Probably better not to speak.

"Either way, if it's below fifty degrees, you wear a coat."

"'Kay."

He raises an eyebrow, and I squirm.

"I mean, yes, Daddy," I say with a little extra sugar in my tone.

"That's my good girl."

My insides melt and suddenly I'm not so nervous anymore. My Daddy will take care of me.

He runs his hands up the back of my thighs until he

reaches my panties. "Here's what's going to happen. I'm going to get you changed for bed, then I'm going to put you over my knee and lower your training panties to give you a very sound spanking. After that, you're going to go stand in the corner with your red bottom on display for ten minutes. Then, Daddy will snuggle you to sleep. Tomorrow, you're going to sit at the kitchen table and write down ten things you love about yourself and you're going to repeat that list to me every day this week while we stand in front of the mirror together. Any questions?"

Uh, yeah. Like, why is my clit throbbing over everything he just told me? But I don't ask that because I'm not sure if I'll get into more trouble for having sexual thoughts instead of thinking about how naughty I was, so I shake my head.

He kisses me again then rises and goes to my dresser. "Go potty while I find some pajamas."

I scurry into the bathroom, glad for a moment to cool down. After using the toilet, I wash my hands and stare at myself in the mirror. I'm flushed but my skin is glowing, and I look happy.

"Little girl, quit stalling before I add more spanks," he calls from the bedroom.

Whoops!

He's sitting on the bed waiting for me. As soon as I'm close enough, he pulls me between his thighs again, then reaches under my dress and hooks his thumbs into the waistband of my panties. I hold onto his muscular shoulders as I step out of my big girl panties and into the training ones he chose for me. The thick padding between my thighs instantly makes me start slipping into my younger headspace.

When he pulls my dress up and over my head, I suck in my tummy. He shoots me a stern expression as he leans forward and unhooks my bra.

"One of these days, you're going to understand just how beautiful and perfect I think you are and you're not going to be nervous to be naked in front of me. I plan to replace all that bad shit in your head with only good stuff," he says as he helps me into my nightie.

His reassurance soothes me, and I believe him. "Thank you, Daddy."

"You're welcome, Little bear. Now, let's get this over with so I can snuggle you."

I squeeze my thighs together in anticipation, the padding of my panties making me feel so naughty and Little. When he takes my hand and effortlessly pulls me over his powerful thighs, I let out a whimper.

"Naughty Little girls get spankings on their bare bottom," he says as he flips up the back of my nightie and pulls my panties down.

One of his arms bands over my waist. When I try to wiggle against his hold, I realize he has me firmly in place and I'm not going anywhere. Crap.

"Anything you want to say or talk about before we start?"

With a heavy sigh, I shake my head. "No, Daddy. I'm ready."

Smack!

Oh, holy moly, I wasn't ready.

Smack! Smack!

"Oomph!" I start kicking my feet.

This spanking is nothing like the fun one he gave me before. He starts off hard and fast, alternating cheeks, peppering my entire bottom all the way to the tops of my thighs.

"Ouchie! Owwie!" I cry out.

I try to squirm and kick but his hold on me is unrelenting as he continues to spank me with powerful swats that heat my bottom from warm to sizzling hot and stinging.

"I'm sorry, Daddy! I'm sorry!" I practically shout, my

words coming out in pants as my body fights against the punishment.

He ignores my pleas and spanks me over and over again. At one point, I kick so hard that he pauses and throws his leg over the backs of mine. I'm truly pinned in place with no way to escape.

Well, that's not true. I can say my safeword. He told me I could use it during punishment but even though it stings and I'm fighting against it, I don't think I want it to stop. I think I need this. It's something I've wanted for so long. Because this spanking is coming from a place of caring on my Daddy's part and he's doing it as a way to teach me a lesson that I really do need.

Tears well in my eyes and start to spill down my cheeks while I continue to squirm and wiggle against his hold. Finally, a sob breaks free from my chest, and it feels like a dam broke because my tears are coming out in big fat drops as I let it all out. All the emotions I've had over my body, my condition, my marriage. It all pours out of me.

I don't know when the spanking stopped or when he moved me up to sitting in his lap with my head buried in his chest, but it feels like home. He strokes my hair and rocks me against him.

"That's my girl. I'm so proud of you. I know that was hard. Let it all out, baby. Give it all to Daddy to shoulder," he murmurs softly.

So I do. I cry and cry and cry until I can't squeeze out another tear and then I snuggle into him, completely and utterly exhausted. I also feel lighter than I've felt in years. It's euphoric.

He doesn't say anything for a long time. He just holds me, and we sit quietly. When he finally pulls me away from his chest, he wipes my cheeks and kisses my forehead.

"You're so damn strong, Little bear."

My smile is watery. "Thank you, Daddy. I really think I needed that."

"I think you did too. Your punishment is almost over and then we'll crawl into bed and cuddle, okay?"

I groan. Standing in the corner sounds like less fun than the spanking. He just chuckles and sets me on my feet.

"Nose in the corner. Arms at your sides, holding up your nightie so your bottom is on display. Ten minutes."

With a dramatic sigh, I shuffle toward the only open corner of my bedroom. My panties are still bunched at my thighs so it's a slow walk and, when I finally get there, I glance back at him. He gives me a nod, so I turn my nose toward the corner and grab hold of my nightie to hold it up. Then I stand there for what feels like nine days, seventeen hours, and forty minutes before he calls me over to him.

I practically leap from the corner directly into his lap, which makes him chuckle as he wraps his arms tightly around me. I immediately feel like I'm home. Not because I'm in my house. My home is in this man's arms. It's where I'm meant to be, and this is what love is supposed to feel like.

24

JAXON

"Leah Elizabeth Day, if you don't stop trying to touch my cock, you're going to find yourself over my knee again getting your bottom rewarmed."

My girl lets out a long, dramatic sigh as she yanks her hand back. After her punishment was over, I tucked her into bed next to me, slid her pacifier between her lips, and told her it was time for bed. She has other things in mind.

"But, Daddy, I wanna play," she replies in a sugary sweet tone.

I tighten my arm around her. "Little girls who just got punished don't get to play. It's bedtime, Little bear. Go ni-night."

She sighs again. "I don't know if I can sleep."

With a growl, I roll on top of her, pinning her to the bed. "Then maybe Daddy should fuck your pretty little mouth and give you that pearl necklace I promised you."

Her breath hitches. Even in the dark room I can see her bobbing her head. It makes me chuckle. This woman is going to kill me.

"You want that, baby? You want me to slide my cock

between your pretty lips and use your mouth for my pleasure? Because even if I do that, you still don't get to come."

"Please...I want that."

Fuck. I am truly fucked. In one swift move, I get up and flip the bedside lamp on. "Scoot over to the edge of the bed and turn your head my way."

She obeys as I pull off my underwear, my cock already rock hard.

"Take your nightie off so I can play with your pretty tits while I fuck your mouth." I fist my cock as she scrambles to obey, leaving her only wearing her training panties. Her nipples are hard points just begging for my attention.

She turns her head to face me as I take a step forward and bend my knees slightly to guide my cock into her mouth. God, she's so beautiful. The way she looks at me like I hung the damn moon makes me feel so powerful. I'll do anything to make my girl happy and keep her protected. Anything.

The warmth of her mouth makes me groan. "Fuck, baby. You feel so good. Such a good girl. Suck it in deeper."

I'm pleased when she obeys and hollows out her cheeks until I hit the back of her throat. When I lean forward and take one of her nipples between my fingers, she moans and lifts her hips in response. Her legs are bent at the knee and she's squeezing her thighs together. I know I shouldn't let her come so soon after being punished but fuck, I want her to come apart with me.

"Is your little pussy wet for me, baby?"

She bobs her head as she continues to suck my cock, gagging every now and then when it hits the back of her throat.

I slide one hand into her hair and fist it, holding her head still so I can thrust. She whimpers and moans as she sucks while I fuck her warm, wet mouth.

"You're so perfect for me, baby. Such a good girl."

One of her hands snakes down her tummy but I grab hold of her wrist before it reaches her pussy. She lets out a soft whine.

"Naughty girl. You don't get to touch your pussy without my permission. That will be one of your rules we'll discuss tomorrow."

Sweat coats my skin as I fuck her mouth, pushing a little deeper with each thrust. She's moaning and gagging, saliva leaking down her cheek as she tries to keep up. I'm so close it's painful, but I don't want this to be over yet because she looks so beautiful like this.

"You want Daddy to come all over your mouth and chest?"

"Mm hmm," she hums around me.

Fuck. She's perfect for me. So perfect. I tighten my hold in her hair. "Hold on, baby, Daddy's going to fuck your throat nice and hard. Tap my leg three times if you need me to stop."

I place one of her hands on my thigh and thrust into her mouth roughly as my climax barrels through me. My entire body tenses. As hot ropes of come start to spurt from my cock, I pull out and shoot my seed all over her mouth and chest, groaning loudly with each pulse.

My pounding heart and ragged breathing are the only sounds I hear as I float back down to earth and see my girl using the tip of her index finger to spread my come around her chest like fingerpaints.

"What are you doing, Little bear?" I ask with a chuckle.

"Painting, Daddy."

I throw my head back and laugh because this woman just continues to surprise me. "I'll be right back. Gonna get something to wipe this up."

She's still *painting* when I return with a wet washcloth and clean her up then press a kiss to her swollen lips. I get rid of the cloth and help her back into her nightie before climbing into bed beside her.

She immediately snuggles up to my chest. "That was really fun, Daddy. I want to do that again soon."

"Okay, baby girl. It's time to sleep."

I slide her pacifier between her lips and turn off the bedside lamp. We lie in silence for a long time while I stroke her back in slow circles. Her bottom is pressed against my cock, and I can feel the heat from her earlier spanking still simmering on her skin. It doesn't take long before I'm hard again. There's been enough time since her punishment. It would be okay to give her pleasure. At least that's what I tell myself because as good as her mouth felt, her pussy feels even better, and I want to be inside her.

Slowly, I move my hands up under her nightie and tuck my thumbs into her panties to pull them down.

She giggles and wiggles her bottom against me. "I knew I could break you down."

I swat her ass and chuckle. "Little girl, you're skating on thin ice. Just for that comment I should pull your panties back up and make you go to sleep."

"Noooooo. I'll be good. The goodest. The most goodest girl you've ever seen. See, I'm being good. Now, please fuck me?"

Jesus. I'm putty for this woman. So gone it's not even funny. And I don't care because she's stolen my heart and I know she's going to take care of it just like I'm going to take care of hers.

"Oh, Daddy's going to fuck you. I'm going to fuck you hard and deep until you're screaming my name and begging for mercy."

Jaxon

"So, I know my sister already invited you to Thanksgiving but I want to invite you myself because I would really love it if you came. If you have other plans with your friends that's okay too, so don't feel obligated or anything." I'm rambling but I'm nervous. I haven't brought a woman home to my parents since Wendy. Not until now. Leah belongs in my family, and I know they will love her as much as I do.

We're sitting on the couch drinking coffee. Thanksgiving is in four days, so it's a bit last minute, but I already know in my heart I'm going to spend the rest of my life with Leah Day. She's it for me. There's no one else. We still have a lot to figure out. Hell, we just defined what we were last night in the parking lot of the damn bar. It'll all get worked out in due time.

"I would love to go to Thanksgiving with you. Thank you. Greer invited me to go with her family so I wouldn't be alone, but she'll insist I go with you instead."

Warmth fills my chest, and all I can do is grunt because the lump forming in my throat right now is too thick for me to speak. She smiles softly and snuggles against my side.

After I fucked her last night, we finally fell into a deep, comfortable sleep entangled in each other. It was so perfect and everything I never thought I wanted but now can't live without. This woman has turned my world upside down and I love it.

We spent this morning cuddled up on the couch with cartoons playing quietly in the background while we had our coffee. It's been perfect. Being with her feels so right.

Her phone vibrates next to her and she giggles when she reads the message. When I furrow my brow in question, she shows me the text.

> Greer: Did you get your ass spanked last night?

> Bree: Greer! You can't just ask that! But since she did, did you?
>
> Natalie: Yes, inquiring minds want to know.
>
> Bella: Who got spanked?
>
> Sara: I don't want to know if my brother spanked my future sister-in-law.

I shake my head and chuckle. "I have a feeling you and your friends are going to be trouble together."

Leah's eyes sparkle with mischief. "Absolutely. But it will be so much fun."

Oh, man. I am totally in for it. I have a feeling a few of my friends are in for it too.

"You better tell them the truth. That you got a spanking for being a naughty Little girl so your Daddy had to correct you," I tell her with a wink.

A blush so bright that it makes me chuckle blooms on her cheeks. Her phone vibrates again, and she pulls her bottom lip between her teeth.

"What's wrong, baby?"

She looks at me then down at her phone. "The girls asked if I could go out for a girls' night next weekend with them."

I hate that she immediately worries I'll be upset or tell her no. After setting my coffee on the side table, I reach for her chin so she's forced to look at me.

"I will never keep you from hanging out with your friends. I have guys' night with my friends a couple times a month too. The only thing I ask is that you don't do anything dangerous and if you're going to be drinking, I'd prefer to drop you off and pick you up unless you guys have arranged a designated driver."

Her entire face relaxes as a smile spreads. "So I can tell them yes?"

"Absolutely. I'll be at Dane's house next Saturday night for poker."

When she throws her arms around my neck and hugs me, I'm so fucking happy. This woman is exactly what I've needed all these years, and I can't wait to make her the happiest woman for the rest of my life.

25

LEAH

"What should I wear?"

It's the third time I've asked that question and every time, Jaxon has told me to wear whatever makes me most comfortable.

My closet has become a blur of colors as I stand in front of it with my hands on my hips. It's Thanksgiving and while I've spent every night this past week in Little Space with my Daddy, I don't necessarily want to look Little on the first day I meet his parents.

"Do you want me to pick out your clothes, Little bear?"

With a sigh, I turn to the man I'm head over heels in love with and let out a sigh of relief. "Yes, please, Daddy. I'm just nervous."

He brushes past me and kisses my forehead. "I know, baby. You don't need to be, though. My parents already love you."

I sit on the edge of my bed while he sifts through my closet and eventually ends up picking out an emerald-green cotton T-shirt dress and my favorite jean jacket to go with it. Then he looks through my shoes and chooses a pair of dark brown ankle booties. I'm shocked at how much I love what he chose. For a big lumberjack, he has pretty good taste.

"You finish getting ready and get dressed. I'm going to go over to my house and shower and change. I'll be back shortly," he says as he leans down to kiss me.

"Okay, I'll miss you."

He pauses and stares at me. "I'll miss you too. But you know, I've been thinking. If we moved in together, we'd never have to miss each other."

My eyes bulge out and my breathing stops. It's not that I haven't thought about living with Jaxon. I have. A lot actually. We haven't spent any time apart all week except when we were working, and it's been wonderful. But part of me wonders if it's too soon. The other part wants to live with my Daddy because I know he's the person I'm going to be with for the rest of my life.

"Really?" I squeak.

His eyes sparkle. "Yes. You can move in with me, or I'll move in here. I don't care, as long as I'm with you. Whatever house we vacate, we can make it a rental."

I chew on my bottom lip nervously. Even though I love this run-down little house, his has an extra bedroom and another bathroom. The backyard is bigger, and it doesn't need any of the work that my house does. It would make sense to move in with him.

"I'll tell you what, baby. You think it through. We don't have to rush. It's something we can wait for if you'd prefer. You're it for me, but I'll wait as long as you need. Just know that whatever house we end up in, I want you to make it your home and your safe place. I don't give a shit where I live or what kind of décor we have as long as I get to come home to you. Okay?"

I'm speechless and, when he gives me another kiss and leaves, I can't move for several minutes. This is something I am definitely going to be thinking about non-stop for the rest of the day.

After I finally regain some composure, I get dressed and curl my hair in soft waves then look at myself in the floor length mirror. I look beautiful. Glowing. My hips fill out the dress in a sexy yet classy way. A few weeks ago, I would have hated how I look right now but I have no doubt my Daddy is going to take one look at me and not be able to keep his hands off me for the rest of the day. It's a process, but he's showing me day by day that I am truly beautiful and special. I'm slowly starting to forget all the hurtful words my ex poured into my head.

When Jaxon knocks at the door, I shake my head with a smile because even though we live in this tiny little town with absolutely no crime, he insists on locking it every time he goes to his house for longer than two seconds. I swing the door open, excited for him to see me in the outfit he chose. Only when I do, Jaxon isn't standing at my door. It's Kevin.

"What the hell?" I ask.

He's dressed in a suit, and he looks smug as hell with his overly gelled hair and practiced smile.

"Happy Thanksgiving, babe. You look great. I knew you'd change your mind."

I jolt back, completely thrown off guard. "What? I didn't change my mind. What are you doing here? I told you I wasn't going to Thanksgiving with you."

Annoyance gleams in his eyes. "I texted you and told you I was coming to get you. You never responded, so I took that as a yes."

Laughter bubbles up from my chest. "You took me ignoring you as an agreement? I blocked your number, Kevin. I didn't see your text because I have no intention of going anywhere with you or even talking to you ever again."

His nostrils flair. "I drove all the way from Portland to

come get you. You're fucking coming to Thanksgiving with me."

My mouth drops open.

"No. The. Fuck. She's. Not."

Jaxon's large hand clamps onto the back of Kevin's neck and he yanks him off my porch.

"Hey!" he squeals.

"You must be her lowlife, piece of shit ex who tore her apart. I'm Jaxon, her new man, the one who loves her and is going to help heal all those broken pieces."

I press my lips together to try to keep myself from laughing at Kevin's pissed off yet slightly terrified expression.

Jaxon releases his neck, and Kevin stumbles back.

"Who do you think you are touching me?" Kevin huffs as he straightens his perfectly pressed jacket.

My eyes widen when Jaxon advances until he's only a foot or so away from my ex.

"What's your safeword, Kevin?" Jaxon asks.

Kevin's eyes squint and his eyebrows draw together. "Huh?"

"Nope, that's not it." Jaxon draws his fist back and plows it right into Kevin's face, knocking him off his feet onto the wet ground.

My hand comes to my mouth in shock. I need to put a stop to this because my Daddy might actually kill my ex.

"Jaxon!" I cry out.

He looks back at me and winks, a smirk pulling at his lips. He's in full control of his temper right now, and I don't need to worry.

Kevin groans and moves to get up, but Jaxon stops him by pressing his boot to his chest. Then he leans down and rests his forearms on his knee as he stares down at the man I thought I once loved.

"If you ever come near this woman again, if you ever come to Pine Hollow again, I will hunt you down, and I will

Jaxon

make you regret every life choice you've ever made. I'm not afraid to go to jail to protect my woman. I'd spend a lifetime in there for murder if it means keeping her safe. You get my drift?"

I'm grinning from ear to ear as Jaxon hauls Kevin to his feet by his jacket and shoves him toward his car. My ex is babbling, mostly incoherently, but I hear several insults toward both me and Jaxon that we both ignore as we watch him stumble to the driver's door.

"Oh, and Kevin," I call out. "I took the liberty of sending our divorce papers to your parents along with the hospital records from when you wouldn't untie me. They called me personally yesterday to apologize on your behalf and let me know if I ever needed anything to give them a ring. Apparently they never actually hated me."

His eyes bug out of his head as Jaxon barks out laughing.

"That's my fucking girl," he says as he looks at me with so much love, it makes my tummy flutter.

As soon as Kevin's BMW is out of sight, I run down the steps and into Jaxon's arms. "I want to move in with you. To your house."

He stares at me for a long moment and swallows several times before grunting, "Okay."

I glare. "Okay? That's all you have to say?"

"Oh, baby girl, I have lots to say. Firstly, where can we get some fucking boxes so we can start packing, and secondly, I can't believe you were married to that douchebag."

"I know, right?" I scrunch my face.

I finally get a look at his outfit and my entire body warms. He looks like a hot lumberjack. One who matches me. His flannel button down is the same shade of green as my dress. He looks hot as hell and I kind of want to jump his bones right now.

"You look nice."

He winks. "I look even better with you at my side."

My cheeks heat. "Did you match with me on purpose?"

"Yep. I'm thinking it's going to become a thing. That way everyone knows you belong to me."

Oh, boy. I definitely want to tear his clothes off.

As if he knows what I'm thinking, he chuckles and takes my hand. "Come on, baby. Let's go see our family."

So much emotion swells in my chest. It's been so long since I've had a family. It's a good feeling. Especially with him by my side.

"It was so nice to meet you, Leah. We hope you'll come for dinner again soon." Jaxon's mom wraps her arms around me in a tight hug and it takes everything in me not to cry. It's been so long since I've had a motherly hug like this.

"I'm so glad Jaxon found you. I can see how much he loves you and how happy you two are. He can be a real pain in the ass, but he's a good man," she whispers in my ear.

I smile and squeeze her a little tighter. "He's a very good man. I love him very much."

Then, to my surprise, his dad wraps his arm around my shoulders. "Welcome to the family, Leah."

I'm quiet on the short drive home. Jaxon's parents treated me like I've been part of their family forever from the moment I walked into their warm and inviting home. It was the best Thanksgiving I've had since my parents died. Sara and I are already becoming fast friends and his mom invited me to join her at the town's annual Christmas bazaar in a few weeks.

"Thank you, Daddy," I say when he parks in his driveway.

Jaxon

He looks over at me, his brows lifted in confusion. "For what, Little bear?"

"For today. For being you. For loving me and taking a chance on me. In all the years I was with Kevin, I never felt even an ounce of the love I feel from you."

"Well, I feel the same way, baby. Your love makes me a better man."

When we get out of the truck, he holds out his hand. "Come with me. I want to show you something."

He leads me into his house toward the hallway. When he comes to the first door, he opens it to a completely empty room.

"What's this?" I ask.

"This is going to be your playroom. You can bring as many toys and stuffies into our room as you want, but I also thought you might like a special playroom just for you. I can build some shelves and a window seat if you'd like. We can get a bed so you can take naps in here if you want. You can even invite your friends over for play dates."

My tummy flutters as I look up at him. I can't believe he's this thoughtful. Well, actually, I can believe it. He's Jaxon. The grumpiest, gruff, most thoughtful and caring person I've ever met.

"I love you, Daddy."

He lifts me by the waist so I wrap my legs around him. "I love you, too, Little bear."

EPILOGUE

JAXON

"Text me when you get there and when you're going to leave."

She rolls her eyes, but a smile spreads over her features. "Daddy, I'm only going a few blocks from home. Greer lives like two minutes away."

I raise an eyebrow. "And? Anything could happen in two minutes. A car accident. A deer jumping out from nowhere. Your car could break down. I need to have Dane look at it, by the way, and make sure it's safe."

When she lets out an exasperated sigh, I shoot her a wink. "Can't be too careful when it comes to my baby girl."

We're getting ready for our separate nights out. She's going to Greer's for a girls' night and I'm heading to Dane's for poker night.

"Okay, Daddy. I'll text you when I get there and when I leave."

"Good girl. And if you have any drinks—"

"I will call you to pick me up instead of driving," she cuts me off.

"Sassy brat," I grumble.

She giggles. "We've gone over the rules like five times. I'll be safe. I'll call you if I need anything. I promise."

"Okay. Most importantly, have fun."

Her eyes sparkle as she grins. "Thank you, Daddy. You have fun too."

After I watch her drive off, I get in my truck and wait until I receive a text from her, confirming she made it to Greer's. I'm probably being overprotective, but it feels so damn good to have someone to take care of. I get the feeling she likes it too.

When I get to Dane's, I'm welcomed with a cold beer and several slaps on the back.

"You sure you want to hang with us? This is a single guys' group, after all," Dane says.

I roll my eyes. "Fuck off. I can't wait until you guys start dating again. I'm going to give you all so much shit."

Austin shakes his head. "Won't be a problem for me. I'm never dating again."

Silas and Dane agree with him while Asher says nothing, and Linc and Gage shoot each other a look.

"I saw Summer Pierce yesterday. She was picking up groceries. Is she staying next door with her mom?" Cole asks.

Dane grunts. "Yeah. She arrived two days ago."

"You talk to her?" I ask.

He shakes his head. "No. We haven't run into each other. Greer told me."

Linc snorts. "You live next to her mom and you haven't run into her? So in other words, you're avoiding her."

"I'm not fucking avoiding her," Dane snaps.

"Dude, what the fuck happened between you guys?" Silas asks.

Jaxon

Dane scrubs a hand over his face. "It's a long story."

We all stare at him, waiting.

"We're here all night, asshole. Get to talking," Gage finally says.

We sit in silence as Dane sighs, his jaw flexing.

"You know how she grew up. Her dad was the town drunk. He spent every dime and dollar on liquor. Everyone treated her and her parents like they had the plague because of him," Dane says before he chugs the rest of his beer.

We sit and listen as he continues his story. Even though we've all known Summer for most of her life, I don't think any of us realized how bad her childhood had been. When he finishes talking, we all let out curses.

"You think she'll ever forgive you?" I ask.

Dane shrugs. "Not sure it matters at this point. Once she gets things figured out with her mom, she'll move back to the city. I doubt we'll even see each other while she's here."

I snort because that's wishful thinking on his part. Dane bought his parents' house when they moved into a smaller one story because his dad couldn't climb stairs any longer. Summer grew up right next door and was Greer's best friend. He's delusional if he thinks he won't see her. I don't tell him that, though. He'll just have to figure that out himself and I can hardly wait to dish some shit out to him like he did to me.

LEAH

I'M HAVING the best time with my friends. We've been sitting around the fire pit in Greer's tiny backyard for the past several hours talking and giggling non-stop. Greer's best friend Summer moved back into town and joined us. She's just as sweet as the rest of them. I have a feeling she and I will end up being good friends.

"Okay, we've waited long enough for the juicy details. Spill, Leah," Greer says as she spins her marshmallow over the flame.

"Whatever do you mean?" I ask.

They all burst out laughing.

Natalie points at me. "How was Thanksgiving?"

My shoulders start to shake as the memory of my Daddy punching Kevin comes to mind and I spend the next half hour telling them all about it. This is possibly one of the best nights of my life. Though I have a feeling I'm in for a lot of best nights in my future.

Jaxon hasn't texted or called since his simple *Good girl* reply when I let him know I got here safely. It's such a breath of fresh air being able to hang out without getting a million insecure texts or calls. I miss him, though. We've only been apart for a few hours and yet, I want his arms wrapped around me.

"What's that look on your face?" Bree asks.

I grin because I can't help it. I'm truly happy, and I feel like it's radiating from me. "I miss Jaxon."

Natalie, Bree, Greer, and Summer are all grinning like fools at me, and I can practically see hearts in their eyes.

Greer smirks, her eyes sparkling. "Let's go see him then."

My face scrunches. "What? No. I'm enjoying girls' night."

"We can still enjoy girls' night. While terrorizing the guys. I think they're due for a prank." Greer waggles her eyebrows.

Natalie leans forward and claps her hands. "Oooh, I'm so in. What should we do?"

We start throwing ideas out. Toilet papering. Silly string. Water balloons.

I snap my fingers. "I got it. Do any of you have a suction cup dildo?"

Their attention turns to me, and they listen to my idea, wicked grins spreading over their faces.

Greer has a whole drawer of sex toys—including several suction cup dildos—which is perfect. We all pile in one car and make a quick trip to the store in search of what we need then make a stop at Jaxon's house before heading to Dane's.

We park a block away and, as we're making our way toward his house, we're all trying not to giggle hysterically.

"Shh! They're going to hear us before we even get on the porch!" Natalie hisses.

Willie trots beside me on his leash, excited for whatever we're doing even though he has no idea he's about to be a prop in our stunt. The pocket full of treats I have is enough to make him join in on the fun.

Bree and Summer hide behind a tree in the yard while Greer and I make our way up to the porch to set things into place. Natalie sneaks around the side of the house.

"It's probably weird that I'm putting my dildos on my brother's front door," Greer whispers.

I burst out laughing, covering my mouth with my hand to try to keep quiet. "Let's just hope he doesn't touch them. You might need to get rid of them after tonight."

She shrugs. "Meh, I have a half dozen more."

My body is shaking uncontrollably as I try to hold back more laughter. "Remind me to ask you later why you have so many sex toys."

Greer waggles her eyebrows. "A girl can never have too many toys."

I tie Willie's leash to the railing of the porch and slide his eye patch into place before I drop a handful of treats in front of him. "Stay, buddy. I'll give you more treats later."

"Ready?" I ask.

"Ready!" Natalie hisses from the corner of the house.

I give Willie a kiss on the forehead before Greer and I leap off the porch and run to where Summer and Bree are hiding. Natalie starts tapping on the closest window.

We're all giggling as we wait. Willie is on the porch happily munching on the snacks I dropped. When no one comes, Natalie taps again, louder this time.

Suddenly, the front door swings open and the suction cup dildos nearly smack Dane in the face as he steps out. Jaxon and Silas are right behind him, followed by the rest of the guys.

"What the fuck?" Dane thunders.

Jaxon looks at the dildos, which have big googly eyes taped onto the ends, then notices Willie on the porch. His eye patch also has a googly eye taped to it.

"Jesus!" Jaxon growls.

Silas, Austin, Dane, Cole, Gage, Linc, and Asher are all looking at Willie and then back at the dildos in confusion.

"Dude, why the fuck is your dog here?" Silas asks.

Jaxon looks out toward the front yard, a gleam in his eye, and I start wheezing as I try to keep from laughing out loud.

"Because my Little girl likes to make fun of my one-eyed Willie."

Suddenly all of his friends start laughing. The corners of Jaxon's mouth twitch, and I love that he's fighting against laughing too.

"Little girl!" he calls out.

The five of us practically fall over as we burst out into giggles. Jaxon hears and strolls over to the tree, plucking me up from the ground. When he throws me over his shoulder and starts smacking my bottom, I laugh harder.

"You are such a brat," he grumbles but I can hear the laughter in his voice.

"He didn't want to be a one-eyed Willie anymore!" I cry as he smacks my butt several more times.

Jaxon

My friends stumble out from behind the tree, and Natalie appears from the side of the house.

"What's with the dildos?" Dane asks as he reaches for one.

Greer squeaks. "They're mine!"

Dane's hand freezes and his eyes widen. Austin raises an eyebrow as he peers at Greer in what can only be described as eye-fucking.

"Jesus! Get these fucking things off my door!" Dane yells. "Fuck, I need to replace my goddamn door now. Why the fuck do you have these? You're my sister!"

The five of us laugh harder. Dane looks like he might vomit, Austin is still staring at Greer, Linc and Gage are grinning, Silas is untying Willie, Asher is standing on the porch shaking his head, and Cole is looking at Bree in a way I've never noticed before. Her cheeks are bright red under his scrutiny and it's adorable.

Jaxon still has me slung over his shoulder. "What am I going to do with you, Little bear?"

I giggle. "Probably spank me a lot, but the look on your face was so worth it."

He smacks my bottom again. "Oh, you're going to get so many spankings. The first one will be tonight because where is your goddamn coat?"

Whoops! Forgot about that in all the fun.

When he finally sets me down, I look up at him and slide my arms around his neck. "I missed you and wanted to see you."

Our lips meet for a brief kiss.

"You could have just come and joined us for poker night, you know," he grumbles.

I shrug. "Yeah, but this was so much more fun."

"We're renaming the dog," he declares.

Willie lets out a bark and we both start laughing.

"Nah. I really like your one-eyed Willie. Besides, he has two eyes now."

Jaxon glances at his dog, who still has the patch on with the big googly eye attached. A slow but sexy grin spreads across his lips. "You're going to make me so gray."

I giggle. "Yeah, but I'm also going to make you the happiest man in the world."

When he shakes his head, my smile falls.

"No. You're not. You already have, Little bear. Life doesn't get any better than this."

Relief floods me, and I hug him close.

"Come on, brats. Let's go inside before you all freeze. Where the fuck are your coats?" Dane asks.

We all start laughing as we file into the house, and I don't miss the way Summer glares at Dane as she walks by. He just raises an eyebrow at her in response. Huh. I need to ask her about that. Seems like it might be an interesting story.

Jaxon takes my hand and leads me inside with Willie trotting behind us. When we're in the warmth of the house, I pause and look up at my Daddy.

"What?" he asks."

"I just love you. And I'm so happy I moved here."

He wraps his arms around me and pulls me into his chest. "Me too, baby. Me too."

KEEP UP WITH KATE!

Sign up for my newsletter get teasers, cover reveals, updates, and extra content!

ALSO BY KATE OLIVER

West Coast Daddies Series

Ally's Christmas Daddy

Haylee's Hero Daddy

Maddie's Daddy Crush

Safe With Daddy

Trusting Her Daddy

Ruby's Forever Daddies

Daddies of the Shadows Series

Knox

Ash

Beau

Wolf

Leo

Maddox

Colt

Hawk

Angel

Tate

Rawhide Ranch

A Little Fourth of July Fiasco

Shadowridge Guardians

(A multi-author series)

Kade

Syndicate Kings

Corrupting Cali: Declan's Story

Daddies of Pine Hollow

Jaxon

PLEASE LEAVE A REVIEW!

It would mean so much to me if you would take a brief moment to leave a rating and/or a review on this book. It helps other readers find me. Thank you for your support!
-Kate